VENUGOPAL ACHARYA has an honours degree in Economics and a Masters in International Finance. He is a teacher, a practicing monk over two decades, and an author of three highly acclaimed books.

His recent best-seller, ***Are You Connected- 25 keys to live, grow and succeed with self and others,*** is published by Penguin India. In this self-help book he shares practical skills that help us connect better to our own selves and improve our relationships with others.

To read his writings and hear his talks on mental hygiene and spiritual development, visit www.yogaformodernage.com

Cricket in a Monastery

Monks' Secrets Reveal Sacred Life Lessons...

Venugopal Acharya

VISHWAKARMA PUBLICATIONS VP®

Cricket in a Monastery

1st Edition Published in India by Vishwakarma Publications in Feb 2018.

ISBN - 978-93-86455-44-4

Disclaimer
This is a work of fiction. Names, characters, places and incidents are either the product of the author's imagination or are used fictitiously and any resemblance to any actual person, living or dead, events or locales are entirely coincidental.

Published by:
Vishwakarma Publications
283, Budhawar Peth, Near City Post, Pune- 411 002.
Phone No: (020) 20261157
Email: info@vpindia.co.in
Website: www.vpindia.co.in

Cover Design : Abhishek Patil

Typeset and Layout : Gold Fish Graphics, Pune.

Printed at : Repro India Ltd., Mumbai

₹275/-

To all my uncles (dhodappas) and aunts

Author's Note

This is a work of fiction.

Over the last nineteen years I have lived in a monastery, and therefore friends may suspect a resemblance to some incidents from our ashram. However, I honestly maintain that the story line in general and the characters in particular are purely imaginary.

It's natural that the place I live in can influence the plot. Hence I confess that this book is an attempt at creative visualization, and candid self-expression. I sincerely assure that no identification-either direct or an allusion- of any actual persons, places, incidents, and buildings is intended, unless explicitly claimed by me.

Although the story is fictitious, the incidents quoted from the history of world cricket are true.

Part 3, chapter 12 contains stories from the temple town of Udupi. The town and the names and incidents concerning the swamijis of the temple are true inspirational examples.

❑ ❑ ❑

Acknowledgments

I offer my heart-felt thanks to His Grace Bhurijana Prabhu, whose loving instructions and blessings made this possible. He told me to 'write a story every day, even if it's only one sentence', and that led to this book.

I offer my deep gratitude to Srila Prabhupada and Radhanath Swami for giving me spiritual shelter. I feel indebted to Govind Prabhu who believed in me and encouraged me to write boldly and confidently.

My sincere thanks to Gauranga Prabhu and Sankirtana Prabhu, as their love and affection infused fresh enthusiasm in me. Chaitanya Charan dasa's friendship and timely guidance helped me add a crucial section in the book. Gaurgopal dasa, Shubha Vilas dasa, and Siksastakam dasa have been great friends, whose trust and belief in me gave me the strength to write this story.

Thanks to Sneha for editing the manuscript. Vishal Soni and the team at Vishwakarma Publications have been kind and supportive during this project.

Siddhesh Bharti and Abhishek Patil helped design the cover of the book. Thanks and love to you both. I offer my deep appreciation to Mr Maheswari, Raj Chopra, Krishna Gopal, and the team at

Gopal's Garden High school for kindly giving me the facility to write this book.

My special thanks to Ashok, Viki, Rupali, Vrushant, Disha, Lalit, Vineet, Prashant, Sandeep, Jaydasa, Pravin, Vikas, Darak, and Rajesh for their confidence in me. My friends in the ashram, namely, Manohar, Dauji, Hare Krishna, Mathura Mohan, Sri Chaitanya, Gopinath Chandra, Prem Kishor, Damodar, and over a hundred and fifty more, have showered love and forgiveness on me. I hope and pray I continue to always receive their affection.

I remember with gratitude and love, my wonderful parents, family, and cousins- the gadibidis- for their profuse affection and blessings. My brothers' good wishes and my grandparents' love sustain me.

I thank each of you reader for accepting this offering. I intend to serve you, and may this story entertain you. I beg you to please keep me in your prayers, today and always.

❑ ❑ ❑

Contents

PART 1

Venky's Dilemma

PART - 1

CHAPTER 1

Is it Ok to Love Cricket?

March' 2011

"Cricket is our religion and Sachin is our God" read the banner, loud and clear. Venky sighed, "I have chosen to be a monk, and the place I stay in, no one ever talks cricket." The world of India outside the small ashram where Venky stayed with sixty other monks, lived, breathed, slept, ate and drank cricket!

The ashram however was indifferent to the Indian craze. "We have our own craze," wondered Venky, as he returned alone from the fruit market looking at the many hoardings when the Sachin bill board caught his attention. His heart churned with emotions, "We get up at Goddamn 3.30 in the morning, and have our prayers, meditation, classes and yoga till lunch. I hardly have any spare time. Oh, those were the days when I slept till late hours in the morning, and only if a match took place in Australia or New Zealand I'd be up so early."

Lost in thoughts of the world cup held in Australia in 1992 when as a twelve-year-old he had prayed intensely for India to win the cup; he had wished Sachin won it for India.

He then recalled how as a five -year- old, his first impressions of cricket were from the Benson Hedges cup held in Australia when as a mere child he had for the first time seen on TV coloured clothing, flood lights, white balls, and bikini clad women relaxing over a cricket match. At five, he was baptized into the world of cricket by his cricket crazy father, uncle, brothers and his community. His father gave him a bat, and hoped he swung it like Kapil dev or Srikant and if he did something impressive with it, they'd happily share it with their friends. He was the cynosure of everybody's eyes; his older brothers and dad hoped he'd grow to be a cricketer like Vivian Richards but now here he was, washing pots and mopping the floor of a quiet monastery.

Paummm…

He was rudely woken by the honking cabs at the Fort road. Hurriedly looking at his watch, he realized he was late. The fruits had to reach the kitchen in another five minutes where they would be cut and offered to the deities at the temple altar.

The ashram was part of a small temple set up and worship of deities meant cleanliness and punctuality, and he knew he had to rush. Quickly negotiating the traffic at the stop light, he pressed his right hand towards the slowing cars, and ran forward although the signal showed red. His own saffron clothing of traditional *dhoti* and *kurta*, attracted curious looks ever since he had donned them five years ago. In India people still respected this colour connecting it to renunciation, and austerity.

Venky was a monk now, and was respected in his ashram and the community for choosing to live a life of renunciation; his leaving home meant giving up even cricket besides other hobbies that he had pursued while in college.

He had also relinquished a promising career as a manager in a multinational firm. "Oh, you are just on time" exclaimed Mahadev as he pulled the bag from Venky, and began the process of offering the fruits. Relieved to be on time, Venky relaxed, and his thoughts went back to cricket and Sachin. "Oh, that was a great century Sachin scored at Perth on a fast bouncing pitch in 1992…. I remember my brothers partied with rich food and I too had succulent *chole Bature* at the Kailash Parbat restaurant. I felt proud of Sachin then," Venky's grin gave way to a broad smile; he was reliving those happy moments.

"You seem to be on a spiritual high," noted Aki who was passing through the alley of the ashram and had noticed Venky's happiness on reminiscing about a bygone event.

Venky nodded, and looked the other way. He pretended to be busy with something else.

"Maybe I should ask him about my dilemma," Venky thought as he rushed to wash his clothes before the afternoon class. "It's going to be Aki's class today, and in half hour, it would begin."

"Have you stitched the clothes yet?" asked Aki.

"Not yet, but soon" Venky said.

"Both of you are really slow," Aki was now impatient, "Where is Shyam anyway?"

"He's sewing the button of your shirt" said Venky hurriedly, "I have done my job and closed up the holes. He's now finishing it. By evening you shall have it."

Aki moved his eyebrows down and frowned, "I need it fast; maybe I should have done it myself." He then walked away.

"I shall surely ask him today if it's all right to love cricket," thought Venky "and there's nothing Aki doesn't know. He's after all the wise sage of our ashram. Besides, if I ask in class, it might help a few other cricket crazy monks as well."

***

Venky looked at the watch again; it was 3.45 pm. He had washed his clothes and put them for drying on the rope lines where fifty- nine others too dried their saffron robes. The saffron shades all looked the same, yet amazingly each one knew his own cloth, and in the early hours, despite poor light, they grabbed their own set while rushing to the temple to mark their attendance before the conch blew to signal the start of temple services.

"The class starts at 4.00 and I could grab a nap for fifteen minutes" thought Venky, and exhausted from a tiring day, he fell on the hard -wooden floor. This was the same hall that few hours ago served as a lunch hall, and a few hours from now would be the bed room for the monks. During the day, classes and meetings too happened in this modest setting of an ashram.

"Om…." The collective invocatory chant of the ashram mates woke Venky with a start and he sat upright. There was no time to enjoy the stupor; the class began.

"So, Krishna is teaching us to be focused on our path with unswerving determination,"declared Aki quoting Bhagavad Gita 2.40.

"Maybe this is a good time to raise my hand and ask the question on cricket" thought Venky, "or maybe not. What would the others think about me?"

"Yes- no" Venky tossed around inside, while nodding his head demonstrating his attentive presence to the teacher.

Quietly he rose and slipped away to the bathroom, washed his face and ran back to take his seat right in the front. No one ever missed Aki's class; there was wisdom and unlimited satire. He exposed the vagaries of this crazy material world in a way no one had ever done. Ever since he had first attended his classes over a decade ago, Venky had become his fan and his inner quest for the meaning of life seemed to end in his association. Aki had all the answers and the unique ability to present the most complicated scriptural statements in the most simplified manner. And he did it nonchalantly.

Today was no different, yet Venky's mind slipped to the banner he had seen a while ago. There seems to be some big cricket event happening. He could feel it in the air but what is it? The hectic life in the monastery gave him no time to explore the world outside. "I am sure something exciting is happening, but what is it?"

"A spiritualist is indifferent to the mundane affairs of the society," declared Aki in his characteristic style, dismissing the world and its nonsense as if they had no consequence. "Look at our Venkateshwara, he is so happy in his daily service, and so absorbed in his spiritual practices right from 3.30 in the morning till 9.30 pm, I am sure he has no idea that our country is going mad over the world cup."

"Oh, it's world cup time," Venky thought as he found his answer while the class now looked at him, "No wonder, I can feel strong vibrations."

Meanwhile Aki dismissed cricket and continued praising Venky's absorption. "Look, our Venkateshwara is unaffected by this crazy game, isn't it?"

The class burst out into a mild laughter. "Why are they laughing? Are they aware of my inner turmoil?" wondered Venky.

As all eyes were now on Venky, he said somewhat sheepishly, "well, not really, I was curious to know what's happening and I am glad you said it."

Now the monks were uproarious.

"But you are so happy here, aren't you?" probed Aki in front of the packed class.

"Yes of course," confessed Venky.

The class smiled in approval, even Venky felt that the whole fuss about cricket was a silly waste of time. "I mean, how can I ever imagine not living with these guys? Wow! This is an unbelievable spiritual world; everyone is on a high from the time we rise at 3.30 in the morning. The chanting, dancing and singing and then the meditation, classes, and breakfast, everything about life in the ashram is electrifying!" Venky suddenly felt the cricket fever dissolve.

"I believe George Bernard Shaw once quipped that cricket was a game played by twenty-two fools and watched by twenty- two thousand fools" commented Venky. Others laughed and clapped while Aki concurred.

"So, shall we continue our discussions on the Gita?" asked Aki, and the audience was happy he had mentioned cricket in his class.

As the class progressed, Venky pondered on his fluctuating mental state and wondered what was wrong with him. "Maybe I need to ask Shyam first and find out if I am normal! Everyone here is indifferent to this silly game, and they think I am also dismissive about it. But little do they know, my heart beats to know what's happening in the world cup?"

Venky knew he was attached to monastic life, it seemed like a non-stop party ever since he had begun attending the temple services eight years ago as a college student. The spiritual vibrations in the early hours surcharged his consciousness with devotional enthusiasm. He could never trade it for anything else in the world. Even his parents had come to terms with his life choice; to be a monk and serve the society selflessly without expecting anything else in return. He was thirty- one now, young, handsome and energetic. In service, he found deep contentment and in helping others he felt closer to the Lord of his heart. This was his calling, and the monastery he stayed in, satisfied him in every regard.

Except of course his curiosity to know about the upcoming cricket event.

Although his one curiosity was satisfied- it was world cup after all- but loads of other questions rose in his mind, "who's winning?" and "does India have a good chance to win the cup?"

"But first and most important, am I committing a sin in my desire to know all this about cricket?"

It had been five years since he watched television or read the papers. Once on a train ride two years ago, he had overheard fellow passengers discuss cricket. As he chanted the holy names silently, eyes closed and appearing absorbed, he had been attentive to each word they spoke.

He learnt sacred lessons that day; Sachin and Dravid still played for India and Kumble was no longer in the team. But he didn't dare to ask them any details. How could a monk have cricket attachments? And what would they think? Maybe they'd know he was a hypocrite. "I can't let down the saffron colour I wear," thought Venky, and had decided not to pursue the matter. He struggled that night wondering why Kumble was no longer in the team. But the next morning dancing and chanting to melodious *kirtans-* a form of devotional music, in the ashram, gave him a high and he was glad that he wasn't wasting his time on cricket. He was upbeat the entire day, and cricket seemed unimportant when he served quietly and menially in the sacred ashram premises.

However today was different. "This is the world cup and I need to know more." The banner and Aki's revelation had triggered off the old curiosity. His suppressed cricket passion threatened to flood his consciousness once again, years later.

The neighbourhood resounded with echoes of war cries interspersed with stunning silence. There were loud moans and collective sighs. Usually at this hour, the marine drive road would be packed with honking cars screaming at others to move. The vehicles' snail pace and the overburdened city made Venky often comment that the whole city was constipated! "They are desperate to get out but can't."

But today was different; Venky realized a big world cup game was on. He observed only an occassional car moved on the deserted road.

"It's 9.00 p.m. I need to sleep now and get up early tomorrow for my morning duties."

Venky retired but first he needed to use the wash room. While responding to Nature's call, he was instinctively led to adjust the horizontal slats of the louver and he saw men in blue on the neighbour's television screen. Indian cricket team wore a blue dress and even the frosted glass in the bathroom reflected the colour. He knew the match was nearing an end; he felt his adrenaline pumping.

Back on the hard -wooden floor, Venky's attempt to sleep was futile. He decided to stroll in the aisle of the ashram.

Suddenly there was an explosion of emotions from the neighbours. The deafening fire crackers confirmed India had won the game.

Relieved, he felt now he would get some sleep. Just then Shyam hurriedly walked across to his locker but not before smiling at Venky, "India has won a crucial world cup match, and they have now made it to the semi-finals."

"Good for them," declared Venky expressionless, and as Shyam passed by him, Venky smiled and offered a silent thank you to his God, Krishna. As a young boy, he had often prayed before the Indian team's important cricket matches. But he had now learnt that one shouldn't pray to God for petty material desires. One should only pray to execute the Lord's will, and aspire to be a pure lover of the Lord. Asking the Lord to bless the team seemed so silly for Venky and he wondered what would his spiritual master think of him if he learned about his petty cricket attachments?

The next morning was no different;the prayer, incense, and holy chants surcharged the atmosphere and Venky felt there were more people assembled this morning, maybe they want to thank God for India's victory.

But cricket really didn't matter now, spiritual life was much better than cricket, and life in the ashram moved on.

"Are you, all right?" asked Aki during breakfast, "yesterday you seemed distracted during the class. You were not your usual self!"

Venky got candid, "I am actually disturbed by this cricket thing. I mean I am all right but this is like a nagging irritation."

"That's natural," reasoned Aki, "Everyone out there is crazy about it, and the tremors are felt here as well. But nothing serious I assume?"

"Of course, no problem, but I feel guilty for liking cricket. Am I a hypocrite if I love cricket and also talk and practice renunciation?"

Aki smiled. His non-committed responses were only too well known in the ashram. You could never catch him on any controversial question. If cornered, he'd juggle with clever words and leave the questioner more confused.

Venky was persistent, "Aki, I have to confess; cricket is in my blood. We Indians have breathed cricket all our lives, and now can we really overcome this attachment in a few days?"

Aki said, "Are you coming for the class this evening?" Venky nodded. Aki reassured, "I will share an instructive story today and that might placate your feelings."

Venky wasn't sure if this was yet another way to avoid answering the question straight up, but there was no harm in waiting for the 4.00 pm class.

***

Akhilesh was initiated into monkhood way back in the early 1980's, and received the spiritual name Akhilesh Krishna dasa. Devotees lovingly called him Aki, and he was happy and peaceful by nature.

"Materialistic life is looked down upon by the wise sages since time immemorial. Greed and ambition is the very antithesis of soul's true nature." Aki was expounding on the immortal classic, Bhagavad Gita.

"When will he answer my question," wondered Venky while Aki continued.

"We can learn the dangers of being passionately selfish and greedy even from the cricketers. They can teach us many lessons about life."

"Yeah," the class burst into a cheerful applause. The monks loved it. Learning lessons from cricket and integrating it with Bhagavad Gita seemed cool, and so the approval was unanimous.

"When I was in my final year in college, way back in 1981, Australia played New Zealand in the finals of the Benson cup and the Kiwis were chasing 240 odd runs to win the match."

Shyam whispered to Venky, "He's enjoying the narration."

"As the match closed on, New Zealand had a star of a player, Bruce Edgar who scored a courageous 102 runs as the team chased the opponent team's score with six runs needed of the last ball. The packed Melbourne ground watched with bated breath as Trevor Chappell bowled the last ball. Just then, the captain, Greg Chappell who was also Trevor's older brother called him aside and whispered something. The stunned 50,000 plus crowd saw Trevor bowl the last ball underarm. As a result, the batsman couldn't hit the ball above the ground. It was an anti-climax and in poor taste. Even as he threw the ball underarm, there was a loud moan of disapproval from many in the stadium and the commentator Ian Chappel, the oldest of the three brothers screamed out, in brotherly concern, 'No, Greg, you can't do it.' But it was too late, a disgraceful end to an exciting match, all because one man was desperate to win by hook or crook. As the Aussies walked back feeling triumphant, few Australians cheered the victory but most jeered. Trevor walked back to young teenagers booing him, 'we hate you, you are a spoil sport'. Trevor felt devastated, and the incident became such a big scandal that the Australian and New Zealand Prime ministers had to address their

Nations about this 'unfortunate' and 'unsporting' incident that had bought the game disrepute. Greg later admitted to being a victim of stress and exhaustion and regretted his decision. But the damage had been done, and even today decades later the incident is vividly remembered by all who saw it. Greg and Trevor won the match but lost all goodwill that day. And poor Bruce Edgar, his scintillating performance that day is the most overlooked century of all time."

"We are desperate for success and money at all costs. And the result is we cheat, lie and harm others. Our ends justify the means, and we rise and grow only to find ourselves lonely like these cricketers. What's wrong if you lose a game? Life too is a game, sometimes you win and other times you lose. Why get hyper excited about it? Relax and be happy."

The narration by Aki had all monks hearing in rapt attention. "I was a toddler then" calculated Venky and felt sobered by the lesson taught by cricket.

"But how does it answer my doubts? Is this another instance of Aki's avoiding the issue?" wondered Venky.

Later that evening he repeated his concern and guilt about cricket when he saw Aki drying his clothes.

"Cricket is a harmless game," declared Aki. He was now cornered and felt obliged to give a clear answer. "One could play to feel good, have fun and maybe a little exercise. But when lots of money and glamour is added, like in a world cup, cricket becomes a tool in the hands of the dark forces. It's no longer an innocent sport. It's dangerous and evil."

As Venky felt shaken by his assertion, Aki was gone.

"Hmm, makes sense," thought Venky, "but maybe our guruji who is coming soon could throw more light on this and help me."

❑ ❑ ❑

PART - 1

CHAPTER 2

Meeting Guruji

Venky felt lost at the airport. It had been years since he had been here. Today however was special. He was here to receive his beloved spiritual master and guru, His Holiness Abhayananda Tirtha Swamiji who was coming to India after a gap of six months. He would be at the Mumbai ashram before flying to Italy for a conference. Venky knew this would be a good time to ask him about the cricket and spirituality connection.

Swami Abhayananda Tirtha, the spiritual teacher of the ashram where Venky stayed was sixty years old and an internationally renowned figure in yoga and spiritual circles. He travelled widely although based at the Mumbai ashram where Venky served under his guidance. The Swamiji was immensely popular for his masterful discourses on the scriptures and practical guidance to the ten thousand plus congregation of Mumbai that served the various sections of the society. The community had its orphanages, hospitals, schools and food distribution units for underprivileged children and the leaders and followers looked up to Swamiji for guidance. And he was coming to Mumbai.

At the airport, there was an unusual commotion. Cameras flashed, and camera men adjusted positions and the news crew was super alert.

"What is this huge crowd doing here? They haven't come to see guruji, have they?" wondered Venky as he and his fellow inmates kept staring at the door. Any moment now Swamiji would be out.

"Wahh........ho......hey.... auu....eee....," the roar was deafening.

Thousands screamed in unison as a group of young men walked out the airport and the news men and the crowd was desperate to pounce on them. Police and airport security pushed behind the frenzied crowd as the men walked out to a waiting bus.

"What is that?" Venky asked.

Shyam chuckled, "Oh the gods are here, the Indian team is here to play the finals."

Just then Venky spotted Sachin, and almost instinctively waved his hand to call out to his former hero. Quickly regaining his sense and gaining composure, Venky checked his movements but his eyes like thousands of others followed the players until the last member of the team boarded the waiting bus while the traffic came to a halt. And no one seemed to mind. All eyes were glued on the heroes who had brought so much hope to the 1.25 billion Indians. The nation was desperate to feel a sense of honour by seeing their team lift the world cup.

As the crowd cleared after the team left, Venky sighed. "That was close; there was a time when I would go gaga over this but now it seems a distant memory."

"Look guruji is here," Shyam and Aki exclaimed together, and suddenly the small team of devotees from the ashram got excited. Gaur, a friend of Venky rushed to collect guruji's luggage and trolley. Dressed in saffron robes of a traditional *sannyasi*, or a renunciate, Swamiji looked effulgent. His natural smile and pleasing visage defied his age, and just his sight brought loud cheer by Venky and the driver.

Although born as Arthur in Vancouver, Canada, to a family attached to sports, Swami Abhayananda had no inclination for any of the games his family played. His father coached the university's lacrosse team and his two younger brothers played ice hockey and baseball while the third skied. Arthur left home at the age of twenty seeking God in the Himalayas. Learning from the various teachers at Rishikesh, he finally sought shelter with guru Bhakti Ananda Swami, and under his guidance started a yoga school and ashram here at downtown Mumbai. Although not an Indian by birth, Venky's guru had learnt the Indian ways and customs well; he also spoke English in an Indian accent when needed. However, over four decades of familiarity with Indian culture and yoga wasn't enough to hide his fair skin; his appearance anywhere attracted curious onlookers. A white man in traditional Indian sannyasi clothes was a novel sight.

As Venky bent low to touch his guru's feet, he felt a sudden push. In a moment he was thrown on the ground, and hordes of news reporters and cameramen faced Swamiji.

Venky gathered himself and adjusted his clothes and was all ears to the impromptu interview that was about to take place.

"Swamiji, who do you think will win the world cup finals, India or Sri Lanka?" asked one reporter on behalf of all others.

"This is far out," Venky didn't want to miss any part of this. Spiritual teachings dismiss such mundane games like cricket as a waste of time. It's called by many serious spiritual practitioners as Maya- illusion, and has no meaning when the country is suffering so much poverty and corruption. Venky had thought of all these answers when Swamiji spoke after a brief pause.

"I am born and raised in Canada, and the only cricket I know is an insect. But I know Indians love cricket and I love India and its people. And because I love Indians, I pray and wish India wins the finals."

"Yeah," screamed the reporters in joy. Some applauded and there were more questions. But Swamiji hurried to the waiting car while Venky and Shyam quickly jumped on to the back seat.

As reporters pressed for more, Aki indicated to the driver to speed up, and the car soon left the airport.

"I wish India wins the finals," these words from guruji was music to Venky's ears.

There was a hushed silence inside the car while outside the honking vehicles caused a traffic jam. Everyone was silent, waiting for guruji to speak or ask something.

"Hmm..." guruji broke the ice even as Venky and Gaur had been whispering.

"What's up in the ashram?"

The monks in the car huddled together as guruji seated next to the driver looked behind at all of them, "You are packed up tightly like the cars outside. It's a bad traffic jam today?"

"Yes guruji," Aki answered, "Since the cricket teams have arrived to play the finals, there is lot of excitement and unusual traffic."

As Venky, Gaur and Shyam exchanged glances each urging the other to ask some questions to guruji, Aki took over. "How was your travel and what lectures did you give where?"

After all Aki was the senior most member of the ashram and shared a closeness with the Swami like no one else. Often onlookers would mistake them to be friends while in reality Aki was a devoted disciple like the others. Yet his persona gave an impression that he was candid and in control of himself while dealing with the Swami. Many others, including Venky would often falter and get fidgety in the presence of guruji because of the sheer awe that Swami Abhayananda generated. Many world leaders and celebrities, besides thousands of others sought his audience, while here he was dressed in a simple orange dress, relaxing on a car drive with his students from the Mumbai ashram.

Venky and others were in awe of his advanced spiritual position and respected him. They spoke less and unless called for by him, wouldn't disturb him. "After all," they reasoned, "He has important things to do and we and our issues are tiny and irrelevant."

But today in the car, the cricket issue could be raised because the ambience was casual; no serious issues were being talked about.

Guruji was observing the billboards and the traffic outside.

"Who is Sachin?"

This simple query unsettled Venky.

A sudden exchange of hurried glances followed and again Aki came to the rescue.

"He's India's cricket God and is likely to help India win the world cup day after !"

"Oh, Tendulkar!" guruji seemed to know him by his sir name. "It's an interesting poster," he pointed to the cricket is our religion and Sachin is our God hoarding up on the road side.

"Yes, Aki what were you asking?" he then looked back again and spoke casually, "I am happy to be back home. I travelled to many yoga clubs and our international centres and since it was the Gaur Purnima season, spoke on Lord Chaitanya."

Gaur Purima meant the birthday of Lord Chaitanya or Gauranga, who appeared on a full moon day five hundred years ago. He is known by many names and is reverentially worshipped in many parts of India, especially in Bengal and Orissa as God or an ideal devotee,who spread the message of pure love of God. He was golden complexioned, and hence called as Gaura, which means golden in Sanskrit. He induced all to experience spiritual ecstasy through chanting and dancing to devotional chants and kirtans. His activities and teachings during his forty -eight -year life is enumerated in his various biographical works, all of which were amongst the favourites of Swami Abhayananda Tirtha. His appreciation of Lord Chaitanya was well known to his students.

"Lord Chaitanya was born to mother Sachi and is also known as Sachinandan, or the darling son of Sachi. And seeing this poster, I am amused" guruji was now laughing.

"What's so funny about that" wondered Venky silently.

Guruji declared, "Cricket may be your religion, but Sachinandan is our God!"

The laughter lasted a long time. Venky was witness to yet another genius of guruji. He humorously dismissed cricket, or did he?

Venky wasn't sure. "Maybe he's just joking, he has nothing against cricket?"

"When is the final?" asked guruji.

Shyam volunteered, "The day after tomorrow is the match and that's when you are leaving for Italy. Oh, there may be a big traffic jam again that day."

"No way," the wise Aki seemed to know everything, "There will be no traffic at all. The whole country would be glued to their sets. We will drive to the airport in twenty minutes."

Now it was forty -five minutes since they had left the airport and they hadn't covered even half the distance to the monastery. It's taking much longer than usual but it's definitely worth it thought Venky. "Such close association with my spiritual master is so rare and I am glad I came to the airport today."

"Indians are really crazy for this game" declared guruji. "Many of you must be really desperate for India to win?" He chuckled looking at Venky.

"Why me," Venky thought and Aki responded, "He was a cricket buff earlier and now he's a detached monk." Others joined the laughter, and Venky too nervously smiled.

"You were into cricket?" guruji asked in surprise.

Venky flustered, "Err, hmm..yes kind of. But I am glad I am out of it. It's a sheer waste of time."

"Really? How long does a game last anyway?" asked guruji.

"Five days minimum and this world cup thing goes on for almost eight hours each time they play."

Venky knew this was the right time to strike, "Could I ask you one question guruji?"

The Swami nodded in approval.

"Is cricket bad? I mean is all of this a waste of time and *maya*, an illusion?"

Silence.

Guruji didn't say anything.

Venky's mind raced, "Maybe he's aware of the sensitivity of my question. I think he doesn't want to say anything that isn't politically correct. After all his answer could break the heart of many monks who secretly loved cricket. And there are many closely guarded secrets in the renounced order."

Few moments passed before Swamiji reflected aloud, "I think cricket is an innocent sport. It's better to play any sport than to watch it for eight hours. And I see in India everywhere people are playing; even on the railway tracks and beaches and traffic stop lights. They are just bonkers over it. But when money, betting and glamour pours into this simple game, then everything changes."

Some moments of silence passed.

Aki broke the silence, "Ever since I remember, cricket has been a passionate money centred game and players do anything to win and earn money. But I guess earlier it was a peaceful game."

Guruji spoke in a low voice, "All sports were meant to keep us fit and healthy till the bad world of money and sex took over to control these games."

The wise Aki said, "Guruji, interestingly cricket has shining examples of men with noble character."

"Really?" Venky exclaimed aloud.

Since guruji and others were all ears, Aki continued, "There is an Indian player called Rahul Dravid who was in a cricket camp fifteen years ago. The world cup team was to be selected from the candidates of the camp. At the end of the camp, Rahul Dravid's name didn't feature in the final list. His roommate Vikram Rathore, another probable, announced the bad news that both of them hadn't made it. While Vikram was dejected, Rahul silently packed his kit and went to resume his practice but not before smiling at Vikram. Curious, Vikram followed and was surprised to see Rahul Dravid absorbed in his evening practice just after hearing this disappointing news. Vikram asked him if he wasn't discouraged to which Dravid said he was disappointed but not discouraged. In fact, he claimed this would offer him a golden opportunity to make it big in cricket. How? Dravid explained that during the next few months as the world cup would be in full swing, he would also have a chance to play few domestic cricket tournaments that were critical for the team selection for the England tour that was to follow the world cup. And if he performed well in these matches, he could make it into the team. Sure enough, he did well, got into the team and since then has become a legend in his own right. The cricket world respects Rahul Dravid as a great cricketer and a gentleman. He taught us never to give up and remain positive even in disappointments."

"That reminds me of Bill Toomey," said guruji, excited to narrate a similar story.

"He didn't make it into the American Decathlon team in the 1964 Olympics. But rather than get discouraged he was out jogging the next morning and when his friend asked him if he wasn't aware that he had missed the selection, Bill smiled, 'Yes, I know I am not in the team, but I am preparing to get a gold medal in the 1968 Olympics'.Surely four years later, he not only made it into the American Decathlon team, he also won a gold medal for his country."

"I think our monks could learn a lot from this. We live in tough times with so many distractions and temptations everywhere. If we let go of our past failures and keep our vision fixed on the future, we'd also succeed in our spiritual practices."

❑ ❑ ❑

PART - 1

CHAPTER 3

A Fanatic Kishor

The ashram-temple complex was abuzz with excitement; Swami Abhayananda Tirtha was scheduled to give a talk on 'Cricket consciousness v/s Spiritual consciousness'.

Over four thousand youth from Mumbai were expected to storm into the ashram campus by evening. No advertisement and publicity; just by word of mouth people flocked to hear Swamiji's discourses which were rare nowadays. Besides, the monthly youth festival called the 'Yoga of Love' or also known as YOL festival was popular with the Mumbai youth.

"It's a double bonanza, isn't it?" asked Gaur while Venky returned from the shower. The drive from the airport was exhausting and Gaur clarified, "Guruji is here after a long time and the topic he's chosen is also really hot."

Venky smiled at his own cleverness. Everyone knew he chose the topic for the monthly festivals and organized the event. He had received appreciation in the past for selecting topics that were relevant and catchy. Today he was happy knowing that his spiritual master would address over four thousand youth on the cricket madness.

"Come Venky, guruji wants to see you whenever you are free," declared Shyam in an obvious rushed tone, while Aki standing behind him smiled mischievously.

"But why now?" asked Venky.

"He wants you to give him an orientation on today's festival. What is he supposed to speak and when?"

Venky wondered, "Really...... "Really? He has given a lot of YOL talks in the past. This isn't the first time, and he meets world leaders and speaks at premier universities."

Shyam said, "That may be, but he's never spoken on cricket. He was curious to know what you may want him to speak about."

Venky said, "Me? I am nobody. Aki, you could meet up with guruji and tell him about cricket and its relevance to the Indian psyche."

Aki just smiled while Shyam clarified, "In fact guruji was talking to us about the evening program and Aki mentioned to him how you are the main organizer of this event and also quite excited about cricket. He even told guruji that you think our youth are distracted by cricket very much and need help. So now he's keen to meet up with you before his speech and get some guidance on what to speak."

Venky looked disappointed, "C'mon I am a novice, you shouldn't have done that. What guidance can I give?"

"You can figure that out" said Shyam, and walked away with Aki.

"I think Kishor can help you" suggested Gaur, "You know he was a cricket buff and even captained his school and college team that won the Mumbai cricket championship. He can help you."

Kishor was few years older to Venky and had joined the ashram seven years ago. He was busy with his own spiritual practices and teaching services throughout the day. Very few knew about his cricket history and even when prodded, he'd be reluctant to speak about cricket.

Once when Venky had prompted him, Kishor had gravely dismissed the game, declaring it to be a waste of time. "We are monks now,it doesn't behove us to derive cheap thrills from this stupid game."

"But you played with Azharuddin and travelled to Australia and England to play some tournaments. I am eager to ..."

"It's a past I have nothing to do with" Kishor curtly interrupted, "I'd rather not waste my time on this."

With a stern voice, pointing his index finger at Venky, he had chided, "This is the last time you are mentioning cricket to me, and do you understand?"

They had left it at that. But today was different. Guruji wanted to know more about cricket, and who but Kishor would be the best person to help him.

But how to convince Kishor to accompany him to meet guruji?

Venky decided not to hype up cricket lest Kishor gets peeved. Better tell him guruji wants to meet them both and know some basic things about cricket that would help him prepare for the evening talk. After all, who would not want to spend time with guruji.

Kishor was absorbed in his chanting and prayers.

Venky wasn't sure if he should disturb such a peaceful looking sage who had no cares about the sport that had maddened the country. Who could tell that this was the same Kishor who fifteen years ago had been a die-hard cricket fan.

"Kishor, would you mind if I spoke to you for a moment?"

"Oh, Venky, come in" said Kishor, "You must be busy with the festival. What brings you here?"

"It's about cricket, and guruji wants to know something about the game. I will be obliged if you accompany me to discuss cricket with him. I know you don't like to talk about the game but can you make an exception just this one time?"

Venky felt he had stirred a hornet's nest as Kishor with an expressionless face gazed straight back at him.

Venky clumsily broke the silence, "I am sorry, I know your views on cricket, but I couldn't help this time."

"But why me?"

"There's little time to explain. Please come with me and answer guruji's questions."

***

Everyone in the ashram knew Kishor to be a man of few words as he rarely spoke about himself. He preferred to discuss spiritual subjects and focus on his services.

Born in 1973 to a wealthy Punjabi family that was a blend of tradition and modernity, so typical of south Mumbai culture, he played cricket in school and college. This is all that was known to most ashram members. However, Venky being fascinated by Kishor had discovered more; that while in college Kishor also had a beautiful girl friend who was now a top model. He was flamboyant then, frequenting the top discotheques and restaurants with his uber chic friends. Ever since Venky had heard that Kishor had played cricket with Sachin, he was in awe of him. He wished for Kishor to share his experiences with him.

The brisk walk to guruji's room was not without incident. A young man in his mid-twenties ran excitedly to the two of them and exclaimed, "Tomorrow is the finals Maharaj, and we shall win it!"

"We are not Maharaj," Kishor's voice was grave. "We are *brahmacharis,* which means simple celibate monks who serve *sannyasis* and they are called Maharaj. And besides, what's so special about the finals? It's all fixed. India is going to bat second and win the match handsomely."

"Oh sorry," the man sensing Kishor's heaviness hurriedly excused himself.

"That is a tall claim Kishor," Venky couldn't hide his surprise.

Kishor had more to say, "I had predicted this a month before the world cup began. India will win this one and this reinstates the fact that this whole cricket business is a hoax."

"But how do you know?"

They were now at guruji's door.

Guruji's secretary Deepak politely ushered them to the waiting room, "He's in a meeting with the trustees. Should be over soon. Can you please wait?"

"Kishor, pardon my asking, how can you be so confident that such a big tournament as this one is rigged. There are so many countries playing and millions of rupees at stake. It's a scandalous allegation!" Venky hadn't liked the idea that his heroes could be blemished.

"Hmm, you are a child" Kishor dismissed as he closed his eyes to chant his prayers softly.

"Oh yeah, you are the wise all-knowing guy?" Venky couldn't hide his displeasure.

"I am ordinary," Kishor insisted "but I must reveal to you that even the last world cup India won in 2007 was totally rigged. The cricket big wigs were desperate to promote the twenty-twenty version of the game and what better market than India and Pakistan and hence it was all staged to ensure they meet in finals and have a close finish and as everyone was glued onto the game, the capitalists made billions. They have fooled the gullible masses, especially the Asians."

"Oh my God, this is far out speculation," Venky couldn't digest this, "I didn't know India had won a world cup four years ago and there was a twenty- twenty version of the game. But that's for later. How can you make such serious allegations?"

"And dear Venky, I must share something more sinister," Kishor seemed unaffected by Venky's high pitched dramatic expressions.

"Can you guys speak softly?" Deepak lowered his glasses, "Guruji's meeting is just next door and you wouldn't want to disturb him, would you?"

Kishor continued animatedly, "For your general knowledge, even the 1983 world cup that India won defeating the West Indies was fixed! The guys wanted to tap the fertile Indian market and wouldn't it be nice to let them win a world cup. Then you have the Indians hooked to cricket for life."

"I will hear no more of this" Venky said loudly, "It's pointless to talk to a fanatic. And since you are my senior in the ashram, etiquette forbids me to confront you. I can't tell you, but it's a fact; your claims are all utter rubbish."

"Guruji will see you now" Deepak interrupted them.

The room opened and the smiling visage of the elderly Swami greeted them.

"Come in, and take a seat. I don't have much time but need to know something about the game and especially about the world cup finals tomorrow. This is just to keep myself updated as amongst the thousands this evening I wouldn't want to appear totally ignorant."

While Kishor remained silent, Venky blurted out, "Oh guru maharaj, it's pointless, the entire world cup is rigged. It's already decided who will win and it's a gimmick like the WWF matches they show on TV."

Guruji's gaze narrowed and he spoke softly but clearly, "You mean the cricket world cup is all a sham."

A few nervous moments of silence followed.

As soon as he said it, Venky knew he shouldn't have passed such a big judgement on cricket. You can't talk like that to a person like guruji who had a commanding spiritual stature. Venky felt silly at his blunder and he was now angry to see Kishor at ease and composed.

Guruji had more to say, "So you are claiming that these players are all great actors; while they express joy and disappointment as they win and lose, they are conning the world. They could give the best of Bollywood and Hollywood actors a run for their money, isn't it? Do you honestly believe such a theory?"

Venky's voice was now desperate, "Yes, I guess so, that's what Kishor wants us to believe. I learnt from him that tomorrow India is going to win the world cup and all players have been bought."

Though gentle in appearance, guruji's voice was firm and commanding, "And you want me to speak about this in today's class?"

Those who knew the Swami well had shared with Venky that he rarely got angry but when he did, he spoke more soft and slow. His glance was penetrating and now Venky felt for the first time in his life that his spiritual master was incensed at his remarks. They not only seemed silly but worse, it was impertinent to talk to the guru the way he had. He didn't want to speak like that but felt helpless now. The more he tried to escape, the more entangled he got.

"No that's not what I meant, I mean..er"

But he was abruptly interrupted by guruji.

"You may mean whatever you want but imagine the scandal when the media feasts on my remarks that the matches are fixed." Guruji was staring intensely at Venky.

"But why me?" Venky's head reeled with many thoughts and his heart tossed with painful emotions. "I never thought that way, and it's all Kishor's fault. I always felt the game is fair and like guru maharaj even I want India to win the match tomorrow."

Venky saw his guru shake his head and twirl his face as if he was disgusted with his childish theory. He then looked at Kishor who seemed an equipoised saint, and this made Venky more restless.

Guruji pronounced, "I would have appreciated it, if senior monks like you are more balanced and accurate and think before they speak."

Venky wished the ground below him would tear apart and swallow him whole. He didn't want to see his guru disappointed with him. It had never happened in the past and he dreaded this moment now.

❑ ❑ ❑

PART - 1

CHAPTER 4

Beware of Greed

Venky's exchanges with his guru had always been pleasant. Whenever he met his spiritual master, he received abundant affection and embraces. Just his one glance was sufficient for Venky to feel blessed. His persona radiated so much spiritual energy that whoever came close to Swami Abhayananda Tirtha would feel spiritually surcharged. Only the elite few who worked closely with Guruji on important projects faced his wrath and even that was occasional. Guruji was always in control of his emotions and he rarely got upset. Venky had heard his seniors express that only the fortunate few could see Guruji angry and if one was rebuked even mildly it was declared as special mercy. Venky had also spoken about the blessing of being admonished by Guruji but now he was indeed facing it. And he wished he wasn't so fortunate!

This is disastrous. "What will guru maharaj think of me? He may think I am some clumsy, stupid fool!"

Just then Kishor spoke firmly, "Maharaj, the match fixing is not the main issue. You shouldn't even touch upon this needless controversy. What ails the game is greed, and I could share with you documented facts that reveal the insidious role of greed in the lives of cricket players."

"How audacious of him," Venky was now furious but kept his cool. He had already done enough damage to his reputation, thanks to Kishor. Now discretion would be better. Let Kishor enlighten Maharaj the way he wants to. Venky was hurt at what he thought was Kishor's duplicity. " Kishor is playing a different card now. He's realized the match fixing theory won't impress guru maharaj so he's giving some other cock and bull story."

Guruji spoke, "Greed is a universal disease, and I was already contemplating talking about this issue today in the festival. I am eager to know more about cricket and greed."

He then hurriedly pulled a notepad and pen from his drawer, and sat cross legged in front of Venky and Kishor. "Yes, I am all ears, go on."

Kishor spoke, "Till recently, cricket had been an innocent sport and it was said that gentlemen played cricket. But Hansie Cronje changed all that. He played tough and revolutionized cricket. Before him, cricket was fun but he raised the bar. Under his captaincy, the South African cricket team was almost invincible. He came on the field with his laptop; he had detailed strategies to pin down the players of the opposite team. Everyone thought he was a no -nonsense winner, he rarely smiled. People emulated him and envied his success, until one day a harsh reality hit the news stand.

Kishor smiled as he spoke further, "Hansie Cronje was implicated in an ugly match fixing scandal. And investigations proved him guilty. He too confessed and overnight he was banned from playing cricket for life. From a glorious hero, he had turned into a villain who had brought terrible disrepute upon the gentleman's game. People felt betrayed. But that's not the end of the story."

Venky felt envious of Kishor, "Wow!! What a story teller, he has Guruji totally glued. I wish I could have spoken and impressed Guruji like that."

Kishor said, "Few years later in a mysterious air crash, Hansie Cronje lost his life. After he died, newspapers carried a small article briefly mentioning the circumstances surrounding his death. There was no obituary, no memorial or appreciation. Nobody had anything to do with him. This was painful to say the least. If he had died in good standing, I bet the cricket world would have mourned his death and news channels and papers would have dedicated hours and many pages to him. But now that he had been disgraced, he was a nobody, and his death meant nothing to the world. That's how deadly greed is. It obliterates you and all your achievements to nothing."

Just then Deepak rushed in, "Maharaj it's an urgent call from Los Angeles, they want to schedule a meeting with you and the Governor of California, Mr. Jerry Brown. Even the outgoing Governor Mr. Arnold Schwarzenegger's secretary has confirmed his meeting with you in May. Swami Girishananda is on line."

Guruji was staring at Kishor even as he dismissed Deepak with a wave of his hand, "Tell them I shall call later. I am in an important meeting."

Venky felt honoured that he was part of a significant meeting with Swamiji although he wished he was the one educating him on cricket. But he can't repent now, after all he had asked Kishor to come along.

Venky found the whole thing amusing. He had always seen his spiritual master as the all-knowing wise sage who sat on the sacred seat from where he gave discourses. Most of his classes were on scriptures, primarily the Bhagavad Gita. But today the roles were reversed; Guruji was in rapt attention and like a dutiful student, took notes.

Meanwhile Kishor seemed only too eager to educate Swamiji.

Venky now thought of Kishor as a frustrated man. As Kishor blabbered on, Venky reflected deeply, "He has many pent-up negative emotions about cricket. Poor fellow, the grapes are sour for him. Maybe he didn't make it big or lost out on some major break in his cricket career. Now he's blaming the game and dismissing every cricketer worth his name as if he is of no consequence. He's surely disturbed; I wish Guruji sees through this unhappy fellow's frustrations."

Deepak came in again, "Maharaj your lunch is ready, you also need to take medicines after that. And you missed your breakfast today."

"Not now Deepak," Guruji didn't want to miss anything Kishor had to say.

"Kishor is enlightening me on the sacred principles of living."

Venky instantly rose up, "Oh no Maharaj, we can come later. Please do take your lunch."

"No, no I am fine and quite excited, go on Kishor."

Kishor smiled as he spoke further, "Greed has taken a heavy toll on the Indians as well. Both Kapil Dev and Manoj Prabhakar are well known cricketers and so is Azharuddin but all of them are involved in ugly cricket betting scandals and accusations and counter charges. It's a pity that millions of youngsters look up to them as role models."

Venky interrupted, "But Kapil Dev has been acquitted, while it's Manoj Prabhakar alone who's been proven guilty."

"They are of the same ilk" Kishor was emphatic. "Most cricketers come from a simple background and the glamour and fame that the game brings goes to their head. Initially they play well and get a huge fan following. Soon money and women lure them, and then greed and lust traps them to abandon all moral scruples.

"Azharuddin was from a modest Hyderabadi family but became a national legend after his sensational debut where he scored three successive centuries in his first three test matches for India. Soon the glamour bug bit him. He left his chaste wife and got entangled with a Bollywood actress and model, Sangeeta Bijlani and then she found out he was having an affair with another woman and so she too left him. Meanwhile the International Cricket Council, the ICC, the apex body for overseeing world cricket as well as the BCCI, the Board of Control for Cricket in India, banned him from playing cricket for life for match fixing. It's disgraceful that a gentleman's game has been tainted by the misdeeds of unscrupulous men of low character."

"These are strong statements Maharaj," Venky seemed to differ in opinion and turned to Guruji to clarify his point of view, "Azharuddin is a respectable man and he is presently a member of the parliament and is protesting against this indictment. He'll surely come out innocent."

"That's beside the point, he is guilty as of now and he is so audacious that he's now playing the victim card. He's claiming that being born a Muslim he's being discriminated against by the majority Hindus. What a disgusting man!"

Venky felt saddened to hear this. He had seen a lot of reruns of Azharuddin's batting exploits, "What grace and style, no one moved their wrists like him, he could flick a boundary off any delivery. He was too good and bought great delight to the hearts of millions of cricket lovers."

And how could Venky forget that evening at Tanjore International, his family's favourite restaurant where as a young boy, on a dinner outing with his folks, he had spotted Azhar and Sangeeta Bijlani on the next table. The couple was absorbed in their loving display of affection for each other which challenged Venky's family's cultural sensibilities. Never before had Venky seen any couple cuddled so closely together except in movies which he saw only with his family and on the sight of any inappropriate scene, his older brothers would cover his eyes. But here it was for all to see; an icon of his generation, Azhar was whispering sweet nothings into her ears and their faces dangerously moved close to each other.

Seated at the adjacent table, it was difficult for Venky's family to turn a blind eye. While they were considerably embarrassed, he and his brothers enjoyed stealing glances at the couple. His father was disgusted at what he remarked as 'animalistic and low class behaviour' and had asked for another table. He even created a mild furore and made sure the couple knew why he had changed the table. Venky who was sixteen years old then had thoroughly enjoyed the scene while his mother was upset that his father, a principled government officer, was making a mountain out of a molehill. Venky and his brothers had laughed over this for months and whenever Azhar came to bat, they saw father spew expletives at his lacklustre batting and his poor captaincy. Father seemed to love to hate him, while his mother was indifferent to the game. She often chided the other cricket obsessed family members for wasting their precious time watching a stupid game. They all dismissed her as an unfortunate woman who didn't know the bliss that a game of cricket brought.

Suddenly Venky felt Kishor nudge him, and was rudely brought to the present, "Did you hear that, Guruji wants to know your opinion on the game."

This was Venky's chance to make amends. He spoke slowly and confidently, "I don't agree with Kishor, but I have nothing to say because I am not as well versed with the game as he is. My heart says cricketers are nice people. A few may get distracted by the glamour but almost all of them are wonderful people both on and off the cricket field. They are gracious gentlemen- sporting in defeat, and generous in appreciating others. And they love to play for the country."

"I am sorry to interrupt," Kishor was now animated, "They don't play for the country, but just for BCCI. And it's the BCCI that pays an individual cricketer almost a crore of rupees per annum. In addition, they are offered Rs seven lakhs for every test match they play, four lakhs for every one- day match. An individual player's annual income is more than Rs 10 Crores. It's vulgar how much money they make and the BCCI too is minting billions!"

"And if they are indeed so happy playing for the country why do these players demand more money?"

"It's all eyewash; they are hoodwinking the gullible Indian masses that lacks any sense of self-worth or national pride. A victory in a silly game against a handful of equally mediocre teams makes Indians feel euphoric. What a shame."

Venky sat stunned. Kishor seemed much more emotional than what he had imagined. And Swami Abhayananda Tirtha had kept aside his notepad and was simply observing the altercation between two of his disciples.

"It's a serious attack on Indians' passion," remarked Swamiji, smiling and unaffected by the duo's fervour for the game "The whole country is mad about tomorrow's finals and here you are dismissing not just the game and the players, but now you are stretching it too far. You claim the country en masse is foolish."

"Yes," Kishor's exclamation was loud enough for the neighbours to hear, "They are not champions, but mediocre men who are victims of greed and glamour."

Swamiji rose from his seat and pulled up the sacred thread hanging on his torso, over his right ear and circled it thrice.

This meant he'd be going to the washroom.

"Gentlemen, I want to thank you for educating me on the game,

but I need to rush for a few meetings before the big class or as you would like to believe the big 'game' this evening. So, you will have to excuse me."

"Sorry Maharaj," Kishor's voice softened, and gone was his aggression, "I think we disturbed you with all this cricket nonsense."

"No, it's just that I have understood now that cricket is an over glamorised sport with lots of money pouring in and benefitting none except the BCCI and a handful of players."

"Yes Maharaj, and one very important thing I need to tell you," Kishor's pitch rose again, and with a sense of urgency, he spoke fast, "I can prove to you Indians don't love cricket."

"What crazy things are you blabbering?" Venky's outburst was loud. He couldn't be a mute witness to what he now thought was an indication of Kishor's suffering from some mental imbalance. Hence, he had to give him his piece of mind, although he knew he would lose his own cool in the process.

Swamiji seemed unruffled. He quietly entered the bathroom with a smile, "Maybe you can tell me this one last thing after I am back. I'd like to know how Indians don't like cricket."

Deepak rushed in, "Is everything all right? The ashram guys are wondering what is happening inside. Your loud animated discussion is creating quite a stir outside. They are all waiting to know what's cooking?"

"Oh, nothing really," Kishor was back to his controlled self. "We are just on the verge of a major discovery. We'll prove how Indians don't love cricket at all."

"What?" Deepak looked incredulously at the composed Kishor while Venky's sarcastic smile only exposed his deep distress.

"You know, I am going out of this room," Venky was decisive, "I mean I have nothing to discuss on this issue. Please, Kishor you can educate Maharaj on your enlightened realizations."

"Oh, you don't want to hear this scoop" Kishor asked.

"No, I have had enough of this" Venky was now rushing out of the room even as the three of them heard the sound of the toilet flush. This meant Guruji would be out any moment.

"Wait," Kishor's eyes grew big, "You dragged me here, you better wait and what will I tell Maharaj if he asks me about you."

The door moved and Deepak hurried out, exclaiming, "Wait till the guys in the ashram hear your stories. All the best."

Both doors moved simultaneously; while Deepak rushed out, Guruji emerged from the bathroom. Venky observed that his spiritual master was graceful in his movements and speech. His mannerisms and habits didn't even hint at him being a busy man. He seemed to have all the time in the world.

"Yes, please tell me if there is anything else you want to say."

"Maharaj, as I was telling you, Indians don't love cricket. They just love to see the Indian cricket team play with some foreign team and if they win, they get delirious as if they have conquered the world."

"And you were saying you had evidence for the same," Guruji was again probing.

"During the local cricket matches, especially the finals of the Ranji Trophy which is the most important domestic cricket tournament and which decides the squad for the National team, hardly anyone is there at the stadium to watch the match. None of the National team players are known in India until they play internationally. Whereas football and hockey is more popular because even in domestic matches, the stands are full and people flock in thousands to watch these matches. But a domestic cricket tournament has just over fifty people watching in a stadium that hosts fifty thousand during an international match. This shows how cricket is simply an empty fuzz of glamour; there is no love for the game but a desperate sense to feel that we are a great country. Our worth unfortunately comes from defeating a few international teams, and we imagine we are world champions. What a pity."

"Hmm," Guruji was wondering aloud, "Why is it like that?"

"That's because we are good for nothing in sports. We don't win any medals in Olympics except an occasional bronze or silver and that too is forgotten soon. And in hockey and football, we are no force to reckon with even in Asia, leave alone the world. And therefore, we are desperate to have some international success. And cricket offers such an opportunity because hardly any other country plays cricket and if we beat a few of them, we create an illusion for ourselves that we are world champions."

Venky couldn't believe what he saw. Guruji was laughing aloud and Kishor was all smiles. He even winked at Venky as if to say, "Just see my clever analysis of what ails the Indian society."

"But Maharaj, this is misleading information," Venky knew the moment he said it, he was entering dangerous waters. But he considered that he couldn't possibly allow Kishor to get away with such lies.

"The ICC is the governing body of cricket and it has more than hundred members. And for your kind information," he was now looking menacingly at Kishor, "You can check on the internet, cricket is the second most popular sport in the world, next only to soccer. Over 2.5 billion human beings watch cricket. So, India winning the world cup is no mean achievement."

"Really," now Kishor matched Venky's aggression, "Then why is it not played in Olympics. Do Germany, China or US or Netherlands play cricket at international level? And you very well know what would happen to India's fortunes if these countries took up cricket with the same passion that India has for the game. India would have no chance. They are not champions today when it comes to hockey, when once they were the greatest team in the world. Not many countries played the sport then, similarly now when others are ignorant about cricket, India is desperately seeking glory at being the world champion. And by the way the Olympic committee was considering including cricket but the BCCI refused because they didn't want to lose money.

"And cricket is an obsession only in Afghanistan, Bangladesh, India, Pakistan and Sri Lanka. And maybe a handful of other Asian countries. And these countries constitute your 2.5 billion cricket fans." Kishor was getting personal and Venky felt slighted.

"In Australia or England, the top cricketer could travel in a bus or train and no one would care who he was. It's only in these sickly South Asian countries that cricketers are treated as demigods."

"I think I need to rush for a few things now," Guruji looked irritated and Venky once again felt shattered.

Venky felt responsible for causing discomfort to the person he loved the most in life.

Venky always thought of his spiritual master fondly. He dreamt of him giving classes, leading melodious devotional chants and cherished all his personal interactions with him. He knew from his scriptural study that a guru or spiritual master is a representative of God and if one pleases the guru, he or she also attracts the divine grace of the almighty Lord. And besides, that's what the very word Upanishads, the sacred scriptures of the Hindus literally meant. *Upa* meant near and *shad* stands for sitting under the feet of the spiritual master. Therefore, Upanishads are studied under the guidance of one's guru.

But today was an entirely forgettable experience. Far from studying the scriptures with his guru, he had been trying to exhibit his intellect and smartness in front of his spiritual teacher. And what a disaster it had turned out to be. Cricket he realized is a mundane, non-spiritual subject. By passionately discussing such an insignificant sport, he was not only demeaning the sacred opportunity of associating with a spiritually realized soul like his Guruji but he was also risking his own relationship with him. All the years of cordial relations and loving exchanges was now risked at the altar of some cheap egoistic battle with Kishor.

And Venky knew he really didn't care if cricket was not a noble sport after all. He also cared less if Indians loved or hated cricket. He knew he loved his guru immensely and had got himself entangled in this discussion just to please his beloved spiritual master. But the whole thing seemed to have backfired.

"I will really appreciate it if both of you leave me alone now," Guruji indicated towards the door as Kishor and Venky stood perplexed. Guruji called out to Deepak to get his lunch.

"But Maharaj one thing you need to remember for today's evening class is the vice of greed. That could be your one message associated with cricket." Kishor seemed to know how to end the discussion.

"Thank you," Guruji looked straight and smiled fully at Kishor.

"And now do you mind," his eyes gazed at Venky and the smile seemed contrived and artificial, "If you will leave me alone to get my things in order."

Venky's mind rushed through many emotions, "Oh my God, he's terribly upset with me. I am done. I should clarify that I have no issues with cricket. Oh, why the hell did I argue with Kishor? I could have just kept quiet and now Guruji is upset with me. Maybe he is not. Let me try one last thing."

"Maharaj would you be speaking about the victims of greed in cricket?"

With a straight face, Guruji replied, "I am grateful you shared these stories with me. I am not sure if I will repeat them in the class today. But surely these are instructive instances for me to remember personally and guard against this evil of greed. I am sobered and I shall strive to be pure and humble and stay away from greed. Thank you very much." He was now bending low towards Kishor in a show of gratitude and thanking him for his time.

Turning to Venky, Guruji said, "Moreover, you have simply confused me with so many controversies. There's nothing really left for me to speak. I spent an hour with both of you learning that

cricket is a disease even in the ashram." Again, a smile.

It seemed mysterious. "Is he upset or all right?" wondered Venky and considered asking him straight if he had been offended by his presumptuous behaviour. But he knew he had already done enough damage to his reputation and nothing he said or did today seemed to create a favourable impression with Swamiji. Maybe discretion is better for now.

"What a mess I have landed myself in," Venky was to later confess to Shyam about the rendezvous in Maharaj's room. While there are thousands if not millions wanting to get a glimpse of Guruji, here he was, a stupid fool who had messed up his chance.

"I lost it and I will never talk about cricket with anyone. It's the cause of my spiritual destruction. My relationship with my guru has suffered because of this nasty game."

Shyam had lent a patient ear without any comment.

As they quietly left the room, Venky knew he had made the biggest blunder of his life. He had spent a decade cultivating the slow and steady practice of spiritual life and it had begun to bear fruit as his spiritual master had acknowledged him and given him his time.

But now it seemed that he had ruined it all.

"Will Maharaj ever talk to me now? He may consider me as an immature fool. All my years of renunciation have been in vain, my pretence has been exposed." Venky lamented.

❑ ❑ ❑

PART - 1

CHAPTER 5

Guruji Reveals a Secret

The next few hours passed in painful anticipation of an event he wished didn't happen. But he couldn't miss the YOL festival. He was the organiser and the master of ceremonies. But how could he compere the event when he had just ruined the whole thing? How could he face his guru again and that too in an event just few hours after he had insulted him by talking and behaving so childishly? It was a royal mess!

As thousands poured in, the hall got filled much before the usual time. A proof of the growing popularity of Swami Abhayananda Tirtha's discourses.

Swamiji entered and suddenly the three thousand plus crowd fell silent. A hush in the hall. You could hear your breadth. Gracefully he offered obeisances to the deities at the altar and gently rose to occupy his seat. Sitting cross legged on an upholstered, raised seat, he surveyed the hall, looked at everyone and a gentle smile on his visage eased Venky's tension. But he knew Maharaj hadn't looked at him but at all the others. And that made him uneasy.

The class began with the invocatory prayers after Venky made the customary introduction in his aplomb style, drawing applause from the packed audience. Venky was a good public speaker himself and he attributed this to his guru's blessings. Now as he smiled and appreciated his guru in public for having taken out his precious time for addressing the Mumbai youth, he felt tremendous discomfort within. Externally he was spot on but internally he was crying. He felt shameful for his afternoon goof up. He couldn't get over it and after the formal introduction he sat right in the front, cross legged like the others to attend the class. He felt foolish and hoped he could focus on the class.

An hour and half of discussion on spiritual consciousness and with more than four thousand people crammed into the hall, Swamiji spoke nothing much about cricket except that it's a game that Indians love and if they loved spiritual life half as much, India could witness a major revolution in her social well-being. And then he abruptly ended the class, inviting questions from the audience.

"If India has such a rich spiritual culture, why is it not popular amongst the youth?" asked one long haired youth who yelled out his question loud and fast on the microphone.

The overhead speaker amplified the sound but Guruji couldn't decipher the question. The questioner's heavy Marathi accent had further confused him. He looked quizzically at Venky who stood next to him overseeing the movement of the microphone amongst the audience.

Venky bent low to whisper the question in his ear and again the same face of annoyance and irritation stared at Venky. "Is he still upset with me?" But there was no time to brood over this.

Venky repeated the question verbatim to Guruji who also leaned forward to listen. Then again he relaxed on his seat and smiled before answering, "Indian youth is busy with cricket and Bollywood. You have no free time from this."

The audience burst into a spontaneous laughter and applause.

Meanwhile Venky sat down and realized that during the entire class, Guruji hadn't looked at him even once. He sulked at what he thought was a confirmation of his Guruji abandoning him. He pulled his mind back to the class, and although he was broken within, he fought hard to put up a brave front. Meanwhile the microphone exchanged hands and occasionally Venky would rise and lean forward to repeat the question to Maharaj.

Another question: "I feel spiritual life is the antithesis of patriotism. One needs to transcend all material identifications including national loyalties. But living in my mother land, I feel attached to India and get emotional when I hear about any freedom fighter's sacrifice to protect our nation. Can I still make spiritual advancement if I love my country?"

Venky shut off mentally; it was a typical question of a young spiritual seeker and he had heard these kind of questions hundreds of times over the last ten years and he also knew his spiritual master's answers by memory. It was all the same predictable stuff. We need to integrate spirituality and Nationality blah blah…he had answered these questions himself many times.

It was sudden and unexpected.

Venky skipped a heartbeat as he heard a loud "Yes, Venkateshwara?"

"That's my name," Venky realized all eyes were on him. His guru had just taken his name in the class in response to the question.

Swamiji continued, "Even I love India although I am not born here. Who wouldn't love India for all her wonderful diversities and yet united in heart and spirit. So many cultures, so many traditions, dialects and religions galore, yet there is one voice and one heartbeat of the Nation; of love and acceptance. India has sheltered so many people and I know India is the only country where Jews have not been persecuted. It's the most beautiful land on the planet."

The audience heard in rapt attention and then broke to a thunderous applause. Their National pride was vindicated even by a Canadian born Swamiji.

"Does this mean these guys are all fools because they are happy about a foreigner appreciating India? Maybe Kishor is right after all." Venky's head raced through thoughts from the afternoon's discussion. "Just look at them. They are patriotic for sure but their gleeful faces reflect the fact that just because a foreign Maharaj has appreciated and glorified India it increases India's value in their eyes. They really have no self-worth."

And that's when he heard his name.

"Venkateshwara knows I love India, right?"

He had heard his name loud and clear and wondered what he had done wrong, now.

Guruji's eyes looked mischievous; he smiled first at Venky and then at the four thousand crowd. "You know Venkateshwara's association has filled my heart with so much love for India that I now feel compelled to share a secret I haven't told anyone. Do you want to hear, and it's about my love for cricket!"

A huge roar engulfed the hall.

Venky couldn't believe what he heard. "He's got a secret about cricket and it's about me. What the hell is happening?" Now the audience sat in silent anticipation. This was going to be the historic moment. A Canadian Swami loves India and cricket and he's got something to share, presumably a secret.

Guruji got the pulse of the crowd. They were all glued to the wooden floor of the hall. None of the four thousand people moved although the temple room had a capacity of only sixteen hundred.

"Thanks to Venkateshwara I love India so much now that I too root for India's victory against Pakistan especially if it's a cricket world cup match."

The hall blasted in celebration. The applause and laughter lasted over five minutes. India had just defeated Pakistan a couple of days ago in the semi-finals and with this one statement, Guruji had captured the hearts of Mumbaikars.

Venky knew the next morning newspaper headlines would feature Maharaj's comments on cricket. Who wouldn't love to know that even a renowned spiritual leader loved India and cricket and the reference to Pakistan would serve as the icing on the cake.

In the midst of the deafening cheer, Venky looked up and saw that Guruji was glancing at him affectionately. The smile not only eased the tension that had tormented Venky for the last few hours but he also felt an upsurge of love for his spiritual master.

Guruji continued to look lovingly at Venky and then after the applause subsided, he again looked at him and declared on the microphone, "I am so honoured to be associated with Venkateshwara. He has taught me a thing or two about spirituality and life. All of you are so fortunate to be guided by him. He's the true youth leader that the country needs."

Then another round of thunderous applause followed. Venky was at the centre stage and this was unprecedented. "To be appreciated by the spiritual master in front of so many people means Guruji still loves me." Venky felt grateful and as he sat shyly, he lowered his head and tears filled his eyes.

"I request you to kindly stand-up" said Guruji.

As the students sitting next to him urged him to rise, Venky felt embarrassed and delighted simultaneously. Another round of applause followed.

Venky knew this was the most memorable moment of his life. "To be honoured and recognized by Guruji in front of so many means he has forgiven me for my imprudent behaviour."

❑ ❑ ❑

PART - 1

CHAPTER
6

Kishor Challenges Guruji

At 4.15 am the temple lights were switched on. The monks who slept in the temple at night rushed for a quick shower before they came back for the prayer session that would start in half an hour. A second later than 4.57 am meant a red mark on the attendance sheet and that would entail extra community services. Therefore, although in stupor, the monks hurried to mark their attendance.

The discipline was rigid but no one complained because the rewards were satisfying. The surcharged spiritual atmosphere was contagious. Even the most spaced out participant would benefit a little at least.

Many who left the ashram due to their inability to cope with the lifestyle returned after some months or years to meet their friends in the monastery and every one of them confessed that those days of hardship and austerity in the ashram were the best days of their lives. The freedom experienced within the four walls of the ashram was real; while the carefree life outside choked most moderns. No wonder then, that even members of the community with families and social responsibilities would make it a point to frequent the temple for the morning program at least once a week. Few came daily because they knew this was the oasis in the desert of the materialistic world. But today was different.

"Do you realize Venky there are over hundred non-residents here?" Shyam hurried to whisper as members came closer to the door of the altar, waiting for the prayers to commence.

"Hmm. So, what?" Venky was still feeling sleepy after the late-night youth festival. The curtains would open any moment and herald the day's program.

The conch shells were blown thrice by the priest to declare the temple altar open for worship inviting the assembled members to offer prayers and chant collectively. It was a spiritually exhilarating experience for many but for the regulars, it was often a ritualistic affair.

"Isn't that unusual? We generally receive not more than twenty to thirty householders for the morning program but there are so many today. I wonder why?"

Kishor standing next to Venky had overheard Shyam and now he declared, invoking his trade mark cynicism, "Oh that's obvious, today is the world cup finals. And our devotees want to pray intensely for India's victory. Everyone is infected by this cricket madness. Such fools; I just feel sorry for them."

"What are you doing here?" Venky was now alert, "You are usually at the back end of the temple every day. What brings you

here in the front with us lesser mortals?"

"I came because it's very crowded at the back."

The curtains opened and members turned to their right, bent down, then knelt low on the ground to offer obeisance. Then they rose again and while one ashram member led the chant, others joined in chorus. These *mangal aarati* prayers were soothing to the heart and infused one with transcendental energy if they could tune into the spiritual frequency that the combination of prayers, chants, *aarati* ceremony and the incense generated.

Venky however was indifferent to the fact that today was the world cup finals. He was on a high after last evening's program. Maharaj had accepted him the way he is; he felt loved and was at peace with himself.

Meanwhile the group meditation-also called as *Japa*-began and Venky struggled to remain awake. His eyes dozed, and slowly he fell asleep even as he sat in the circle with others. Monks congregate daily in groups, during pre-dawn hours, and softly murmur holy chants. They seek to connect to God as they finger their beads for almost two hours. The *Japa* session was the lifeline of the ashram; every monk knew if he was strong in this practise, he could transcend the challenges posed by the mind.

Aki gently tapped Venky on his thigh, "You are really struggling, go wash your face." Venky rose, went to the washroom and returned. Yet again he slept during the chanting.

"What's the matter with you?" asked Aki, "Half an hour ago you were upbeat, and now you are miserable."

"I was up stitching clothes till late at night, three hours after the festival," moaned Venky.

"I am sorry" Aki said, "We could change your services, if it's taking a toll on your health."

"No", Venky seemed to have been shaken by the proposal. "I love the service, and I am keen to continue. It's just that the last few days have been hectic, and a lot of backlog of clothes. But I promise I'll be all right for the next session."

***

It was 8.00 am, time for the morning class. And it would be conducted by Guruji again as he was leaving for Italy that evening. His last address for the next six months would attract many of his senior students and the older members and leaders of the community. Unlike the evening outreach programs, the morning classes were more spiritual and focused on deeper aspects related to Bhakti yoga and principles of community building.

There were over two thousand members and Venky sitting in the front waiting for the class to commence, turned to Shyam, "I am exhausted; I have no strength left in my body. And so many people crowded into this small hall leaves me more frustrated. They can hear the class online, why do they have to flock here?"

Shyam said, "They too love Swamiji, and just as you are eager for his association, they too are anxious to see and hear him in person."

Venky whispered, "But what the hell is Kishor doing here? He generally listens to the class in his room, through the FM transmission. I wonder what brings him here? He is very enthusiastic today."

Shyam said, "why are you getting on his case. Leave him alone. Has he irked you?"

"No, it's just that he almost ruined my spiritual journey. Yesterday we had a big fight in Maharaj's room and I thought I had upset Guruji and would lose his association and spiritual guidance. Somehow, I am relieved and safe. But I will be careful next time; shall stay away from him."

"*Om namo Bhagavate Vasudevaya*"

The invocatory prayers were followed by chanting of more prayers and then Maharaj removed his glasses after reading the Vedic text and purport to the verse. He was now explaining the instructions of sages that were described in the first canto of Srimad Bhagavatam.

Again, nothing unusual. But the moment the question answer session began, the hall reverberated with a murmur. To everyone's surprise it was Kishor who raised his hand. He sat erect and asked for the microphone.

Venky looked incredulously at Shyam, "What's wrong with him? He is the Mr. know it all, he hardly interacts with anyone in the ashram and in the last fifteen years no one has ever seen him ask any questions because apparently he has all the answers."

"Maharaj, Thank you for a nice class. I had a question regarding the upcoming crazy cricket match this evening." Kishor had captured the attention of the audience. "Isn't this total maya and should we

not stay away from all this mad hoopla?"

Venky gasped while the audience laughed.

Maharaj smiled, then slowly began his answer, "For monks, yes, it's a total waste of time. It's maya- pure illusion and would benefit you in no way. But for grahasthas, the householders, it's not a serious affair. For them it's a trivial event that's in the news. Why do you have to take it so seriously? You don't have to think so much about it. It's a silly game after all. Anyways I wish the Indian team all the best for the finals."

Now the senior members and leaders joined in a cheer but not Kishor; he was one man who seemed displeased.

"But Maharaj," Kishor interrupted.

Venky was startled at first because no one ever cut off Swamiji.

He held Shyam's hand, "This is going to be fun, and it is more entertaining than the scheduled cricket match. Kishor was spirited, "You say it's *Maya- illusion*. If that's so, shouldn't we discourage our members from following cricket? It's not good for us. Many in India have nothing to eat. They are suffering from poverty and here cricket fans are wasting so much money on this stupid game?"

"Dear Kishor, I appreciate your concern," now Guruji's voice changed. He looked grave and then in an expressionless tone said, "But tell me, can you stop people from watching movies or following cricket? We should be strict with ourselves, and lead a life of integrity. But we have to be considerate and sensitive to others' interests and passions. If we dismiss them and what they like, we'd be alienating them. Where is our compassion then? Let's be kind to all, even those who love cricket. And by criticizing cricket so much we are giving it unnecessary importance. Why talk about it so much? Strong aversion to something is another sign of attachment; it's simply the other side of the coin. Indifference is needed, not disdain!"

After a brief pause, Guruji asked, "Does that answer your question?" Silence.

All eyes were on Kishor now. His views on time wasting activities of the materialistic people were only too well known in the community. In his classes, he smashed Bollywood, cricket and politics. And today he looked agitated but Guruji had given a mature perspective to the whole situation.

Kishor nodded and the microphone passed to another questioner.

Ramamurthy was over sixty, a father of five children, retired from government service and his entire family was dedicated to serving the community under various projects. He wondered, since Maharaj had wished the Indian team all the best, if winning the world cup would bring glory to India.

Swamiji replied, "In this world, it's always the same news; only people making the news keep changing. Yesterday someone else won the world cup and today it could be another team. There were riots and revolutions yesterday and tomorrow the same can happen. Election news make headlines world over and new parties and rulers come and go. The river of time flows strong and triumphantly while we get lost in the foaming bubbles.

"And yes, winning the cricket world cup may mean happiness to all of you but it also means that the other nations lost the cup. In this world one man's happiness is another's misery. And with regards to pride and glory, hmm, I don't think India's glory lies in winning a world cup but it's in how much its citizens live a life of service and the extent to which they internalize the principles and values laid down by the founding fathers of this Nation."

More questions followed. Someone asked about distractions in spiritual life and yet another wanted to know how to focus better during meditation practices. Swamiji was uncompromising in his answers; he shattered the popular myths of general populace. He dismissed the popular beliefs that engaging in gratifying our senses would bring happiness. He was cutting through their illusions, yet sensitive and accommodating to all.

It was 10.45 am. Guruji rose to leave the hall. He was scheduled to address the senior counsellors on initiating new educational projects in the tribal areas of Maharashtra. Then post lunch he would be meeting the hospital doctors and reviewing a feasibility report on expanding medical and eye camps in twenty- five new villages in the north-eastern states of India.

Then more meetings, until around eight pm when he'd be leaving for the airport.

Venky put his hand on Shyam's shoulder as they walked out of the hall for breakfast.

"I am fully satisfied" Venky said. "A three- hour thriller movie wouldn't have been more engrossing and exciting to me as this class, and especially the Q-A session. I didn't even realize he spoke for over two and a half hours."

"But I am greedy for more" Venky continued as he ate the hot *kichadi* with his hands, his fingers carefully placed each morsel in his mouth. "I shall also attend the counsellors meeting."

"You aren't allowed to, you are not part of the team," Shyam said.

"I know I am not allowed but I shall sit at the back."

"But my dear Venky, your best friend Kishor will be at the door. He's the secretary to the Executive committee and how will you explain your presence to him?"

"We'll see that later. Let's relish this *kichadi*, I am hungry."

Venky was surprised to see Kishor mellowed down. He didn't stop Venky and the other ten desperate non-counsellors who wanted to attend the meeting to simply bask in the presence of their spiritual master. He let them all in and quietly carried out his other activities.

Later at lunch Venky approached Kishor, "I hope you are all right and not upset with me about yesterday's meeting with Maharaj?"

Kishor said, "Oh no, that's ok. I am so happy for you. He appreciated you yesterday in class and he truly loves you. But as for me, you saw how he admonished me in the class this morning."

"I don't think he chastised you. He just spoke on principles, that's all. He loves you too and that's obvious. You are a senior and well known and trusted by Maharaj to foresee so many of the projects."

Kishor sighed, "But he loves you because you are so innocent and I am crooked and haughty. I wish I was simpler and pure like you."

Venky said, "*Arre nahi*, it's not like that. Maharaj loves all but he trusts few. You are the trusted one whereas I am one amongst the millions he loves. He has faith in your capabilities and gives you more responsibility. Your position is indeed special."

Kishor asked, "*Accha* Venky, tell me, was I impudent in asking such provocative questions. I feel bad that I did that today."

"No, not at all, it answered so many other people's questions as well. And by the way, your *kurtas* are almost ready. I couldn't stitch them for some days, but tomorrow for sure I shall give you."

❑ ❑ ❑

PART - 1

CHAPTER 7

Guruji's Excited about Cricket

The ashram courtyard was filled with men and women, boys and girls, children, elderly and even the curious neighbours and passersby from the street, all waiting for Swami Abhayananda Tirtha to come down the flight of stairs from his room and enter the waiting car. He would be gone for six long months.

Many held garlands to offer him as a token of appreciation and thank him for his brief but meaningful visit. He had answered many questions of the congregation and dealt with managerial and leadership issues. He offered wisdom on vexing issues facing some projects and now he'd be visiting Rome to encourage and inspire his students there and help them improve their services to mankind and God.

Venky was relieved he had made up with Kishor. Kishor's vulnerability and his candid enquiry from Venky who was many years younger in age was a sign that he was not snobbish after all.

"He's a nice person," Venky told his friends in the ashram, "and he's also humble. But he has his own idiosyncrasies like we have ours."

Kishor walked next to Venky who had chosen a fragrant Kadamba flower garland to offer his Guruji. Feeling his gentle tap on his shoulder, Venky looked up at Kishor who was half a foot taller than him. After all, at 6'2 he was a lanky former all-rounder and versatile cricketer who could very well have been in the Indian team that was playing the finals right here in Mumbai. And the Wankhede stadium was just a stone's throw away from where they all had assembled.

The heart of South Mumbai was beating loud like the rest of the country anticipating a victory for the Indian team while Venky and others felt their heart beat for another reason; they were anticipating separation from their Guruji.

All of them would surely miss his kind dealings, his brilliant classes, his attentiveness and patience in dealing with their issues and above all, a genuine concern for everyone.

Venky recalled how during the *Kumbh mela* gathering, at a question answer session, one sophisticated gentleman had asked a probing question to Swamiji. Wasn't he affected by stress and anxiety like all the others in this world. Venky had seen his spiritual master humbly admit that he had his share of worries but it was all for people like him. His suffering was Maharaj's concern and he wished he could help alleviate it. Venky had savoured the exchange, and recalled it often to feel loved by his spiritual master. His Guruji's compassion gave him strength to serve in the monastery. It also helped him be an instrument of his guru's compassion and assist him in his tireless services.

Venky knew he couldn't imitate his Guruji who even at sixty worked more than eighteen hours a day while he, at thirty-one struggled with his basic daily chores. But he was happy to know that he was offering his best to assist his guru in his noble cause to live for others well-being. "What use is a life that is lived for one's own self and has nothing to offer back to this world?" his guru had once told him. He cherished those exchanges and now here he was going to see him off. He like the others would surely miss him.

Seeing Kishor walk up to him Venky said quickly, "Your clothes are ready. It took a long time to sew them. Shall give it you tomorrow morning."

Kishor smiled reassuringly, "That's all right. I am sorry for being so pushy about my *kurtas*. Take your own time."

"You know, you are so hard working and sincere. I am so inspired by you," Kishor said to Venky again. Venky smiled, surprised at Kishor's gentleness.

Kishor congratulated Venky, "You have a fragrant garland for Maharaj; he'll be happy to receive it from you. Did you make it yourself?"

"Yes, but I will be very happy if you offer it to Maharaj as he walks to his car."

"No, you should offer it. You love him and you made it and he'd also feel happier to receive it from you."

"No, I will feel grateful and pardoned by you if you accept this and offer it to Maharaj."

The friendly tug of war with each nudging and pushing the other to hold the garland was seen by Aki who walked up to them and declared softly, "Do you know, India has got to chase 275 to win the match?"

Venky who had so far been oblivious to the finals felt a sudden gush of emotions. Yes, it was indeed the most awaited moment and a bigger shock awaited him when Kishor who was smiling and cordial up until now, suddenly frowned. The cricket agnostic in him woke up as he remarked, "Yes Jayawardene has won it for the Lankans. They put up 91 runs in the last ten overs and India is 31 for two. We are losing. This will do good for the Indians; they deserve to lose."

Aki smiled and retreated and Venky now stared at Kishor who again resumed his peaceful demeanour. Venky wasn't sure whether he should feel shocked or rejoice that Kishor who normally discouraged people from following cricket, knew the details of this match. This meant he was updated and keenly following the finals.

Another emotion that played in his heart was a sense of relief to finally see the human side of Kishor; he is as vulnerable as the others he criticizes. "Or maybe I am simply sad that India is losing the world cup finals." Unsure of his own mental state, Venky struggled to compose himself as Guruji slowly walked towards the car.

He smiled at different devotees lined up on either side of the pavement while graciously accepting garlands from his students and admirers. As he neared his car, Venky again pressed the garland into Kishor's hands, "Please offer this to him. Please for my sake."

"If you insist," Kishor took it and as Maharaj came closer, he garlanded Swamiji and almost immediately Swamiji hugged both Kishor and Venky simultaneously. He then smelt the garland and moved forward. Venky and Kishor rushed to the car hoping to get a last glimpse of their spiritual master before he drove off to the airport.

Meanwhile Guruji stopped to acknowledge others.

As he slowly resumed his walk towards the waiting Quallis, Venky turned to Kishor, "So India is losing huh. Sad?"

"Not really, you know something; it's all fixed and pre-planned. India is going to win it." Kishor smirked and dismissed with a wave of his hand.

"You guys jump into the back seat. There is space just for two." Gaur had grabbed Venky's arm and pushed him inside the car before Maharaj came.

Instinctively Venky caught on Kishor, "Come in, we can be with Maharaj."

"No, I don't think I want to come. I am not sure."

"There's no time to think, just hop in before someone else takes the seat."

Even as Gaur opened the front door for Maharaj, Venky pulled Kishor and before they realized they were seated with seven other devotees in the vehicle.

The car began to move slowly at first with Swamiji waving goodbye and folding his palms to his friends, students and well-wishers outside.

Venky panicked, "Kishor, my bladder will burst; I need to pee."

Kishor smiled, "Sorry, you'll need to hold it for the next hour because we are on our way to the airport."

***

Seeing the empty road Guruji smiled, "We have no traffic today, thanks to the cricket match."

Venky silently observed Guruji. He felt trapped. He desperately needed to use the washroom but there was no way the car would stop now. Surveying the traffic again, Guruji turned his head back at the ashram members cuddled in the back seats. "Who is winning?" Silence.

Venky didn't dare to speak about the game. Kishor sat straight, as if indifferent to the questions his spiritual master asked them.

Aki volunteered, "Can't say Maharaj, the game is evenly poised. Anyone could win."

Maharaj hadn't heard the answer. He was absorbed in looking out of the window. The sodium vapour lights on Mumbai's street poles added incongruent colours to the billboards that shone with LED lights advertising clothes, shampoos, soft drinks, and bank schemes, and each of them featured an Indian cricketer.

Venky didn't know their names and seemed to not care. His bladder occupied his mind, and besides, his Guruji was fully present and blissful in the now. He seemed fresh and not tired at all despite the super hectic schedule he had during the last three days of his visit to Mumbai. There was no jet lag and here he was off to another country with a different time zone. And he was fresh and happy as ever.

As Venky's inner focus slowly shifted from his aching bladder to Guruji's smiling visage, a sudden peace radiated in the car.

The phone rang. "Maharaj, it's for you. It's Dr Shah, he wants to thank you for the morning class." Gaur handed Maharaj his phone.

"Yes, Dr Shah, who's winning the match?" Maharaj's voice was loud and excited.

Venky softly whispered to Kishor, "I didn't know he was so interested in the match."

Guruji began responding to Dr Shah's comments, "Hmm. Ok... yes…uh...yes."

Guruji listened attentively to the last minute medical suggestions that Dr Shah seemed to offer on the other end. Again, Guruji interrupted, "It's all right Doctor, and my health isn't bad after all. I am more eager to know if India is winning the world cup this evening or not."

Again, Guruji heard attentively.

"Really? I shall await the inevitable."

After disconnecting the phone, Guruji looked behind, "you all are truly renounced *sadhus*, and you don't care about this game while the whole country has deserted the streets to watch it." Another phone call by one of the trustees and Guruji was once again enquiring about the cricket match.

"What's wrong with him?" Venky again whispered to Kishor, "Is he mocking our plight? I think he knows we are curious to know about the game, that's why he's asking us again and again."

"Oh yes, he doesn't care. He's just pulling your leg." Kishor dismissed the discussion.

"How is the game played anyways?" Now Guruji's question was deeper.

Venky spontaneously remarked, "I can explain it to you Maharaj."

He then volunteered to explain how the game has eleven players per team and while one team bats the other bowls. Venky was absorbed in his description of the game, excited as he was but suddenly he realized Guruji didn't care. He was busy smiling and looking out the window.

Venky stopped the explanation about the game. He felt stupid talking about the game to his spiritual master who had only feigned interest.

A little while later, Guruji again turned behind and asked, "So who's winning?"

Gaur volunteered, "Maharaj, my friend called, India is in a strong position, but still one can't say. Anything can happen."

"Really, it's so long and uncertain. Oh, how keen I am to know who is winning."

Anxious moments passed and in some time the car reached the airport.

As Guruji got out of the car and a waiting devotee offered a trolley to load his luggage, loud shrieks could be heard emanating from the airport. Was it a bomb blast? Terrorism was not unknown to the city.

A girl aged around twenty- five jumped in glee. A security official hugged his comrade, and passengers entering the airport gate paused to hail India's victory.

Yes, India had won the world cup, and Venky too felt elated but contained his emotions.

What startled him was Guruji's response; he was quiet, his half smile and careful surveying of his luggage was in total dismissal of the spontaneous and loud celebration all around him.

Just minutes before, Guruji had been asking too many questions about the game and it had appeared as if he was really keen to know what was happening. But here he was totally indifferent to the celebrations. Quietly, Guruji walked through the security screen while on his either side and in front and behind, people cried, laughed and howled in joy. But for Maharaj, it was just another day.

Venky felt a gentle hand on his shoulder as all of them caught a last glimpse of swamiji who was now walking to the Lufthansa airlines counter.

It was Kishor. "Do you realize how graceful he is amidst all this madness?" Venky couldn't agree less. "Yes, he seemed so keen to know who was winning and he spoke about wishing the Indian team all the best and all that enquiry during our drive to the airport. And now he's so cool. He's detached and doesn't seem to care about what's happening."

"I have never seen someone so deeply spiritually anchored."

Kishor said, "There is a reason behind all the cricket mania he seemed to encourage. He was simply cheering all of us. He personally doesn't care about the game. Now he's off to Italy. I bet there he'd glorify soccer and win the hearts of his students. But he's beyond cricket or soccer or any other game that's played on this planet. In fact, he's got nothing to do with this world. Just look at him."

Venky and others caught one last glimpse of Maharaj through the glass window outside the airport. Maharaj was now off for immigration formalities and was out of view.

❑ ❑ ❑

PART - 1

CHAPTER

8

Guruji Reassures Kishor

The loud drums and fire crackers deafened Venky.

"Guys, rush in fast, before there is another traffic hold up." Gaur spoke in a frenzied tone. "It's getting wild. We need to rush back to the temple before things go out of control."

Soon their car was negotiating the packed crowd on Hughes road. Almost everyone was drunk and the dance was obscene to say the least. Men, women, children and the old alike jumped vigorously up and down. Pelvic gyrations added a sensual touch to the victory celebrations.

Suddenly a group of young men surrounded the car and screamed a war cry. "Are they celebrating a victory or screaming the death of their loved one?" Aki asked in disgust. The driver slowly manoeuvred the car amongst thousands of people who lined up on the streets to have a bash. Huge Indian flags atop cars, buildings and shops were a common sight. Gaur was driving back, carefully. A small mistake by the driver and if he hurt anyone dancing on the streets, there could be a riot. None of the people outside the car seemed to care who they were or where they were. They were intoxicated.

Venky looked at Kishor, "I am glad I am not celebrating this victory. This is sickening."

The return journey showed the potpourri of Mumbai's festivities; colourful and extravagant. While people living in the slums bought out their drums and danced in abandon, the affluent whizzed past in their Mercedes and BMW's, honking loudly and blasting western music off their stereos. Even the Gujarati women, in their traditional *lehenga-choli* outfit were boisterous. As the monks drove past carefully, Venky savoured every moment of the spectacle.

There were other middle- class men and women who rode on their two wheelers, carrying the Indian flag, gleefully. Children played cricket on the pavements as if to honour their older brothers who had just won the world cup. Girls giggled seated on the back seat of their boyfriend's bikes.

Politicians of all sorts came on the streets announcing on the loud speakers, their prize money for the Indian team and how they had offered special prayers for the Indian team to win the cup. Opportunistic as they are, they capitalized on the frenzy that gripped the Nation. It was nearing midnight and suddenly peanuts seller and balloon vendors were in demand and the business of the roadside eateries thrived. Meanwhile loud fire crackers filled the sky and the city was euphoric.

An hour later as the clock struck 12.00, the monks were back at the temple-ashram premises. Shyam pointed to the group, a middle-aged man with his ten-year-old son, both faces painted with the Indian tricolour and they stood silently and tearfully at the gate. Venky thought the man looked familiar: he frequented the ashram often. But here he was with his junior, both offering reverential prayers of gratitude to their God as India had won the cup.

Just then Venky screamed at Kishor. "My bladder!"

"You were desperate three hours ago," Kishor said casually and then laughed, "You've been in the world cup trance, and have transcended the bodily urges."

"Oh my God, I forgot all about it," said Venky and he slowly, painfully strolled to the washroom.

Minutes later he was back, "I never realized, I was so absorbed in the cricket event that I transcended the body's urge."

"That's called *Samadhi*," declared Kishor, "you often hear about spiritual trance where the spiritual practitioner forgets all bodily miseries and needs. You are just so absorbed in the awareness of the present moment."

Venky had heard it all. He knew about the legendary king, Parikshit Maharaj who was cursed to die within seven days and he chose to absorb himself in hearing Srimad Bhagavatam from his guru, Sukadeva Goswami. For seven days and seven nights the king heard with rapt attention from Sukadeva Goswami, and both were so engrossed in the narration that they transcended the bodily needs of food, water and sleep. While that was a historical incident of five thousand years ago, Venky had felt a glimpse of a similar absorption this evening.

Venky turned to Kishor, "You know I am amazed after seeing Guruji so closely today. He just raised my consciousness to a new high. He was so fully connected to himself, it didn't really matter if India had won the world cup or not. He was just so happy within himself. That's what I want."

"You already have that," Kishor reassured, "You are happy and so am I. We are pure spiritual beings, eternal, full of knowledge and bliss. Somehow, we get covered by myriad distractions of this world that includes cricket or Bollywood or politics and we trade our eternal happiness of being, for fleeting pleasures of this world that only titillate our senses for some time. Guruji simply reminded us that pleasures are external to us while happiness is an internal state, independent of who wins and what happens to us."

"Yes, I realized that," Venky concurred, "Just the way Guruji carried himself over these three days; he seemed to be so much at peace with himself. He was present. He allowed the cricket news to enter his ears. He was attentive to each word we spoke in his room. He was present as he praised me during the class last evening. Then he was absorbed looking at the street lights and the bill boards and while talking on the phone with Dr Shah and while answering questions during the morning class, he was just there. Therefore, when it was time to leave, he left so gracefully. Wow!"

"That's the way to live and leave," Aki said, as he too joined the discussion.

"What's that?" both Venky and Kishor asked simultaneously.

"We need to live in the present, and leave the world at death, also being present, connected to the self and the Lord of our heart, totally at one with our spiritual identity. Then it doesn't matter whether India wins the world cup or not."

"Yeah," Kishor said, "Just like Venky was so absorbed in the present, he forgot to urinate."

"We can't sleep anyways now. The fire crackers and the drums are too loud," Kishor said and then requested Venky, "Why don't you come to my room and we could speak for some time and then you could retire."

Venky nodded his head and both quietly walked to Kishor's room.

Kishor mused in the small room, lit by a table lamp. "It's an odd feeling really Venky, I can't tell you. I am happy India won, but I know my life is different. It's not meant for such petty emotions connected to sports."

"But you seemed so different to me," said Venky, "I always thought you were a no- nonsense monk who cared less about any sports leave alone cricket."

"Shh," Kishor urged, "Speak softly, our neighbours are sleeping."

A thin plywood door separated the rooms of the seniors in the ashram. Most of the younger monks, including Venky shared the open ashram space for sleeping.

"What makes you think I am attached to sports or cricket?" Kishor probed.

"Let me be honest," said Venky, "You were vulnerable. You looked a little disturbed at the cricket event. I thought you were getting nostalgic. After all you played cricket and must have wished for India's victory at the world cup so many times but now as a monk you were confronting your own desires with what was expected of you."

"Yes Venky, I must confess I was agitated by the world cup finals. I was all right till yesterday but the fact that the match was held so close to our ashram, at a stadium where I myself played for years and I hadn't missed watching a single match there, and right there we had this mega event and I wasn't part of it. I was torn inside but knew it's insignificant. I knew the hollowness of it all but was recalling my own past dreams and desires from a bygone era. I had wished so often for the Indian team to win the cricket world cup and when it finally did win the cup, I wasn't there. I was miserable yet I feel comforted now."

Venky smiled, "You are disturbed as well as at ease, an amazing contrast."

"Yes, and the reason why I am happy is because Maharaj gave amazing classes. He just accepted us for what we are. He appreciated cricket and wished India wins and he also came down to our level. He didn't judge me or anyone else for wanting India to win the match."

"All this time I was in denial. I was criticizing people and the game for no reason. It was simply a covert attempt to hide my own desires. But after seeing Maharaj so amazingly deal with this issue both in his room where we met him and in his public classes and now in the car, I am convinced it's all right to love cricket. I am a classic victim of cognitive dissonance- a conflict of what I think is right, and what I want. Both are different. Ever since I moved into the ashram, I have felt guilty for loving cricket and following the game. But I couldn't help it. Just before going to the airport I blurted out the score. I couldn't keep it a secret. I had been hearing the commentary on my small radio but was terribly pained that I had been doing it. But Maharaj has eased my pain. I feel accepted.

"A deeper issue has been addressed here by Maharaj. I have been staying in the ashram since 1998 and I must confess I am happy but at the same time pained because I am realizing a deep problem facing not just the monks but also the people outside; it's the inability to accept themselves or others for what they are.

"People need to be kind to their own selves and forgive themselves. It's all right, we are not perfect, we need to approve of ourselves and accept ourselves just the way we are. No need to beat ourselves down for not being exemplary monks or for not being the perfect husband or wife. My dealings with families have revealed to me a common obsession plaguing people; striving for perfection. They want to be perfect themselves and wish their spouse too is perfect. This leads to an inability to accept each other and we build walls instead of bridges. Individuals are like tiny islands that need to build bridges to connect with each other. But we are often so unaccepting of who we truly are that we fail to accept others also for who they are. Each one of us is unique and we need to embrace that and stop being so hard on ourselves and others.

"That's profound," Venky sighed, "To accept ourselves and others."

"Yes and this realization came the hard way because I couldn't accept myself and my hobbies after I joined the monastery and therefore I have felt disconnected ever since I joined the ashram." Kishor moaned softly.

Venky continued to murmur, "That could be a big controversy. I hope you haven't revealed this to others. Not all can appreciate this."

"No, you are the only one I have confessed to, besides guru Maharaj."

"My dear Venky, ever since I chose to be a monk, I had to confront everything that I thought was natural for me."

"Just days before joining the ashram I thought of seeing Sachin Tendulkar bat once, for I knew my inner calling would drag me here and then I might never see Sachin play. I got a special pass for watching Sachin play for India against the Australians at Brabourne stadium and I was amazed at how he scored two hundred runs in just one day, and that was his first double century," Kishor's eyes beamed with joy as he recalled the event.

"But the tragedy was I couldn't enjoy the match. I saw him bat but was also doing my *pranayama*, reading spiritual books and silently meditating simultaneously, while also trying to dismiss the game as an illusion. It seemed so unnatural but I was doing it nevertheless. And I was happy he smashed Shane Warne all over the ground, and it was a scintillating knock, a true masterpiece. Yet I was miserable and felt guilty for wasting my time. That's when my conundrum began and only now, so many years later, Maharaj has alleviated my misery and solved my dilemma."

Kishor continued, "And I wrote an email to Maharaj about a week ago about my predicament," Kishor's voice was now hurried. "I wondered what ailed me. I am successful; people respect me and think I am a great realized monk, but I realized I am disconnected from myself. I asked Maharaj about the reason I feel a vacuum deep within my heart and I admit his reply soothed my troubled mind."

Venky exclaimed aloud, "What? You wrote to him and he replied in the middle of all his intense schedules?"

"Shh," Kishor pulled his hand, "Remember the sound can be heard in the next room."

"It's all right. Anyways it's time for them to wake up. I am eager to read what Maharaj wrote."

Kishor pulled up his laptop and opened the mail.

Venky read out Swami Abhayananda Tirtha's reply.

Dear Kishor, please accept my heartfelt good wishes and blessings.

Your sincerity deeply touches my heart.

I am happy to see you seek true connection to yourself; you seek self-acceptance, and self-love.

And yes, we feel a vacuum in our hearts when we are disconnected with ourselves.

The Mahabharata explains we are miserable in life because we focus our lives only on eating, sleeping, mating and defending. And these four activities are common to animals as well. In fact they do it even better than us. Only when we seek to go beyond these propensities, only when we seek to tap our inherent human potential of making the right choices, do we connect to a higher reality, and that's when we find purpose and fulfilment in life.

You are now at a stage in life when you can no longer live with pretence. You want honest connection, meaningful relationships, and a deep sense of meaning to life. That's a reasonable expectation from yourself.

I have always seen you as a spiritual seeker and now you can choose to raise the bar. And if this means you'd have to leave the ashram, I encourage you to do so. My love for you is not dependent on your being in the monastery. Your humility in expressing your limitations touches my heart deeply. I am happy for you because you are now deeply realizing the need to connect. Yes, as you slip, rise and march on in life, you'd make sense of it all.

Having lived in this monastery over the last thirteen years, you have the exceptional fortune of seeing this world from different perspectives. Your own personal struggles, travels, reading and spiritual practices will help you go deeper, and examine your aspirations and dreams. And I pray that along with your improved awareness, you'd also have the courage to accept yourself the way you are.

Please learn to be a little more kind and gentle on yourself. Practice self-compassion before you 'save' the world.

I also feel grateful to you for rendering such simple services in the monastery. I am aware how you, Venkateshwara, and Shyam have pleased all other members in the ashram by menial tasks like cleaning toilets, stitching clothes, and cooking lunch. I am glad to read about your realization that stitching kurtas of other monks brings more fulfilment to you than earning millions of rupees for a selfish cause.

I thank you for writing to me and giving me a chance to serve you and share with you my humble thoughts on this.

I feel blessed to have known you.

Your servant,

Swami Abhayananda Tirtha

The duo shared a prolonged silence while a few of the neighboring monks slowly moved to the common bathrooms. These monks rose early and practiced their prayer sessions much before the others woke up.

Venky felt sobered, "Do you realize it's 3.30 am. You think it's a good idea to catch up with some rest before the conch blows. They are not going to delay the morning session just because we won the world cup."

"Yes, good night," said Kishor, "We shall churn this discussion some more another time."

❑ ❑ ❑

PART 2

Life Lessons from Cricket

PART - 2

CHAPTER 1

Cricket in the Bhagavad Gita

The next morning, a Sunday, the temple hall was packed as usual. Hundreds began pouring in at 4.30 am, and within two hours there were thousands.

Venky and Kishor both struggled to remain awake during the *Japa* session. The late- night discussion up at Kishor's room caused sleepiness. Aki gently woke up Kishor, who in turn nudged Venky.

Aki said, "It's embarrassing you guys are sleeping in *Japa.* The congregation is observing you senior monks struggle. What will they think?"

Venky said, "That we were up watching the world cup finals, is what they will conclude. Who cares anyways?" Venky was visibly irritated at the repeated nudging.

"It's 7.30 now, remember we are going to Mr Lal's house for *satsang,*" Aki reminded them.

Lal was a 61- year old, senior congregation leader who visited the temple daily at 6.00 am. The ashram looked up to him with awe because he stayed a good two -hour travel away from the temple. He walked up to the railway station and boarded the first train early morning and at 6.00 he was there to chant his *japa* with the monks. He managed his business expertly so that he could retire early in the evening and rise by 3.00 am and be there at the temple for the spiritual program. He frequently hosted spiritual-social get-togethers at his house where a few monks would give a lecture while the other guests listened in rapt attention. The congregation would chant, worship and ruminate over a nice feast of rich Gujarati cuisine cooked by his devout wife and her friends.

Venky smiled now.

"You seem to be happy at the prospect of going to Lal's house." Aki said.

"Who would not?" said Venky, and a moment later quipped, "When we visit his place for spiritual gatherings, the congregation enquires from us 'what's the topic' and we ask, 'what's the menu.'"

Shyam said, "The train ride is the price we've to pay for the lunch feast. And besides, two hours travel one way means rubbing shoulders with the Mumbaites crowding into a packed train coach. There's barely any space to move. Most hang on to the bars inside the coach and last time I inadvertently landed up smelling others' armpits."

Aki had the statistics, "Over seven million Mumbai residents travel in these trains daily and an abnormal number of fifteen passengers occupy per square meter of floor space during the peak hours."

"Oh, lucky we are travelling on a Sunday morning," Venky smiled again. "The trains would be empty today."

"Who all are coming?" Aki asked assertively leading the walk to the railway station as Shyam, Venky, and Kishor hurried to catch up.

"The four of us, that's it," said Shyam.

Shyam was twenty- four years younger to Aki; he was born a year after Aki joined the monastery. He frequently ran errands and was ever submissive to render any chore asked of him. In conversations he generally remained quiet, not wanting to breach the etiquette of speaking before his seniors. He considered it audacious to speak unless asked to. Timid and ever- conscious of his being a new member of the ashram, he was liked by all. Many pulled jokes on him, and he didn't seem to mind that. On the contrary, he loved the attention he got, considering it as a sign of blessing and love.

Besides, the service allotted to him and which he loved, was sewing clothes for the *brahmacharis.* He always carried his needle, thread and the clothes that needed to be stitched. Venky assisted him in this service. Both had learnt this in the ashram as part of monastery training. Sometimes the needlework kept them busy the entire day. Today seemed an exception.

Shyam paced ahead of the group and was ready with the tickets, and soon the four of them waited for the 8.31 fast train to Virar.

"Just look at these miserable people," Aki the wise one spoke, "Has the world cup victory last night made any difference to their lives?"

The station was dirty and smelly, a few stray dogs slept carelessly on the benches while a couple of beggars shared platform seats to smoke *beedis.* It was a dull Sunday morning, and an occasional man or woman walked by on the platform. No one was running. The week-long passion for catching a train and rushing to office and back home, by a frenzied Mumbaikar was now replaced by a laid-back attitude. The station was practically empty.

"They couldn't care less that we won the world cup," Kishor pulled up some sweets and savouries left over from the festival and offered to the beggars who indifferently put it inside their cloth bag that was unusually bloated with non-essentials.

As the train pulled up and the four of them comfortably got their seats, Venky couldn't help smiling at the sight of some passengers sleeping on their back with legs spread out.

"This is a premium space of five seats each one of them is occupying, and yes they all look so frustrated and miserable. The world cup victory hasn't eased their worries one bit."

"It has only temporarily given them relief, like that of a painkiller," said Aki.

Venky looked outside the window of his speeding train and in an instant, pulled away his face in disgust. His eyes caught men squatting, lined up on the tracks; a common pastime of the Mumbai slum dwellers was to respond to nature's call on the railway tracks.

The foursome dozed and fell on each other's shoulders repeatedly.

An hour's ride up north was uneventful.

Aki said aloud to no one in particular, "They are lonely in this world, beset with insecurities and anxieties. Oh, the cricket lovers of this country, if only you knew you are in a mess..."

"That's the typical cryptic Aki," smiled Kishor who had woken up a few minutes ago.

"And knowing Aki, the mystery will be unravelled soon, maybe within the next few days," said Venky.

"What mystery are you talking about?" asked the innocent Shyam and he was ignored by all.

"Why days, maybe today, at Lal's house, Aki has something to share," Kishor said smilingly. He seemed to know Aki better than the others.

Aki was quick to note that Shyam was side-lined.

Aki asked, "Shyam, you have been here in the ashram for two years now. It will be interesting to know how you got here; what inspired you and also what's your take on cricket?"

Shyam appeared taken aback by this question, "Oh, nothing really important. My story is so insignificant."

"That's all right, we'd like to hear nevertheless," said Venky.

Shyam said, "Actually, my passion for cricket had blinded me but one day in these very local trains of Mumbai I got my spiritual enlightenment."

"You just dropped a bomb," exploded Kishor.

"When you hear my story, you'd know what really a bomb blast is!" Shaym said confidently.

"Wow! That's interesting," Venky announced, "Everybody thinks our Shyam is an unassuming guy with nothing worthwhile to share. And no one for sure would think you knew a game called cricket even exists, leave alone having a passion for the same. But I guess as they say, 'every sinner has a future and every saint a past', so we'd now be the fortunate ones to hear his story."

"Oh, we have reached Virar," Aki declared to the group. "On the way back to the temple, remember Shyam, you have to tell your story."

***

The house was filled with guests; the members of the congregation had arrived earlier and decorated the house and the altar with fragrant flowers and frankincense burnt on a metal container. The fragrance and happy atmosphere was a welcome break for Venky and his gang after the foul smelling, stinking experience of the streets and station outside.

"I guess you too are celebrating the world cup victory," Venky's tongue in cheek remarks drew laughs from the crowd while Aki walked up to the raised seat to give his discourse.

Garlands were offered to Venky and the other monks and Shyam as usual shied away but couldn't resist the honour.

"This is the Indian custom, a worship for the colour of the cloth," Kishor whispered to Shyam. "Don't take it personally; it's not you they worship, but the saffron colour. Tomorrow if you leave the ashram, none of these people would care to show respect. Indians, you know have a tradition of respecting *sadhus*- saintly people. But they don't love you for who you are, but what you wear. Remove the cloth, and you area nobody."

Ching...ching...ching...Aki played the cymbals softly, while Kishor beat the *mridanga* drum cautiously. This was the invocatory prayer before the class.

"This is how the householders try to spiritualize what is essentially a social, mundane gathering," Kishor offered his two bits of wisdom to the quiet Shyam.

"You are spoiling this innocent guy with your cynical remarks," Venky chided Kishor.

"*Om*..." Aki was about to start the class.

Mr Lal took the microphone, "Ladies and gentlemen, I am happy to introduce the speaker this morning."

Aki protested, "All of you have known me since the last twenty -eight years."

Mr Lal bent low in respect to Aki and said, "Since I have invited many neighbours today and guests and family members, it will be nice if I introduce you."

"Akhilesh Krishna dasa is a senior leader in Swami Abhayananda's ashram and is also the President of the ashram in Mumbai. He is a qualified engineer from the Prestigious IIT and a MBA from the reputed IIM Kolkata. He decided to dedicate his life to the sacred mission of spirituality..."

Mr Lal spoke for over five minutes while Aki kept his head low and his visage grave.

"He is praying silently", remarked Kishor to Shyam, "He doesn't take any glory for himself but transfers it to his spiritual master and the Lord. A true *sadhu* considers himself a humble servant, nothing more."

Aki now began the class, while Venky's sleep deficit, accumulated over the last three days was now taking a toll. He dozed off while Kishor pinched him on his thigh.

Aki announced, "Today we will discuss the first verse of the Bhagavad Gita."

Venky with his eyes closed now jutted forward, then woke with a start and again his eyelids closed as he began swaying sideways.

"It's embarrassing Venky," Kishor raised his voice in an attempt to wake him up but it did little to subdue the onslaught of sleep. "These are new people, what will they think of you and us, come on, go wash your face in the bathroom."

"The first verse of the Bhagavad Gita relates to our present cricket scenario and the world cup simply echoes the mood and sentiments of what's stated in the Gita." Aki was now loud and clear.

Venky suddenly sat straight, eyes wide open and beamed, "My sleep's gone forever. He knows my pulse."

While Kishor and Shyam couldn't help smiling, the audience mildly laughed. Aki had caught their attention and last night's celebration was still fresh in everyone's memory.

"What a genius," Venky said softly to Kishor.

Aki began his narration, "To know how the first verse of the Gita relates to cricket, we need to know the character of Dhritarashtra well. He spoke the first verse of the Gita and he truly represents a common Indian mindset. There is a Dhritarashtra in every home." Venky's mind raced to the television mega epic Mahabharata which he had seen as a ten-year-old every Sunday morning with his family and neighbours who joined in large numbers to watch each of these episodes. Television was a rare luxury those days and the serial served as a festive event for the neighbourhood.

Dhritarashtra was born blind and hence denied the right to rule the kingdom of Hastinapura. His place was taken by his younger brother Pandu. Hierarchically, Pandu's five sons, the Pandavas then had the right to rule the kingdom. However, Duryodhana, the oldest son of Dhritarashtra contrived evil plans to kill the Pandavas. Dhritarashtra, although appeared to be cordial and moral and even declared that Pandu's sons were equally dear to him, silently consented to his son's wicked ways. Pandavas escaped the attacks, primarily due to the help of Krishna, the incarnation of Lord Vishnu who always helps his devotees.

Eventually the clashes between the Pandavas and Kauravas; sons of Dhritarashtra- led to a devastating war. Just before the war, Dhritarashtra enquired about the preparations for the war from his secretary Sanjaya. Sanjaya narrates to him how the chief Pandava warrior Arjuna is being instructed on sacred life lessons by Krishna who plays the role of Arjuna's charioteer. Their conversation popularly known as the Bhagavad Gita is as intriguing as the plot of the Mahabharata war that culminates with a victory for the Pandavas.

Dhritarashtra's personality has been a fascinating subject for discussion in many Indian homes. His lack of congruency inside out, his external sermons on morality but internal weakness and blind affection for his evil son was the root cause of this terrible family feud.

Venky like the millions of other pious Indians had heard since childhood, many discourses, read books and seen dramas on the Mahabharata. Dhritarashtra was a well-known character, yet it never ever dawned on Venky that he could represent an Indian mind set, leave alone draw parallels with a cricket lover.

Aki asked the audience, "What emotion does the first verse of the Gita primarily reveal?"

Shyam raised his hand. He knew the answer but Aki expertly ignored him and looked at the others.

"Shh...it's not for you to answer," Venky pulled his hand down, you are an insider, friend. You live in the ashram and are well versed with the scriptures. This is a test for the others in the audience."

"Love and concern," said one bespectacled middle -aged man. "The first verse is a question by Dhritarashtra to Sanjaya on what's happening in the battlefield between his sons and the sons of Pandu. This shows he is concerned about the impeding war."

"You are right technically, but there is more to it than what meets the eye." Aki said.

Again, silence for some time.

"Insecurity and fear," answered Aki, himself.

"All these years he had been declaring that his nephews, the Pandavas were as dear to him as his own sons, yet now, just before the war, he makes a discrimination. He is exposed when he asks what's happening between 'my' sons and those of Pandu. Dhritarashtra's duplicity is now open for all to see. He is the silent villain, the real wicked one.

"The lesson to learn is; our pretence can't stand the test of time. If our inner thoughts and external behaviour are not in sync with each other and we pretend to be who we are not, then one day the inner thoughts overpower our external persona to reveal the true self, and we stand exposed in front of the world. Remember if our inside is not the same as outside, the inside would take revenge one day."

Venky smiled at Shyam whose face turned pink.

Shyam whispered nervously, "Did you tell him?"

Venky moved his head sideways and half closed his eyes in a reassuring gesture. He then moved his fingers on his lips to indicate a close secret that they shared.

A week ago, Venky had sneaked into the Accounts office and found Shyam all alone there. The sudden presence of Venky had unsettled him, and right there Venky saw the latest Sportstar magazine, Shyam had been reading a cricket story. On the screen of his computer, a cricket match replay was on. Shyam had been exposed!

He clumsily rearranged everything and claimed he was just touching upon the news. Venky had smiled and ignored the issue, and even once joked about it. Shyam would turn sheepish whenever Venky threatened to tell Aki about it. It was a harmless joke they shared.

Now Dhritarashtra's pretence being exposed made sense; both Venky and Shyam could relate to it while Kishor sat expressionless facing the speaker.

Venky's thoughts raced to that night six years ago when as a young apprentice in the ashram he was caught by the kitchen in-charge. Earlier during the day, a rich feast had been served when Panditji, the head cook had prepared the sweet rice which was happily savoured by all. While others prompted him to serve Venky, a new inmate, Venky felt shy. As others happily urged him to have the rice, he excused himself by saying that he didn't have much of a sweet tooth. He knew he was lying. He was trying to show that he was beyond the enjoyment and satisfaction that food brought. He wanted to give an impression that he was a no nonsense *sadhu*, one who controls his senses and avoids rich and fancy food. However, he had wanted to eat the sweet rice. He had been tormented by his decision the moment the word "no" had slipped out of his mouth. Later as the monks retired at night, Venky had stealthily gone to the kitchen, picked up the remaining sweet rice from a pot, and finding himself all alone had begun devouring it. Just then, Panditji had walked in and was amused to find Venky eating. He had been caught red - handed. Panditji had teased Venky about it for a few days thereafter.

Now as Aki spoke about the principle of 'inside taking revenge on the outside' Venky nodded his head in agreement; he had a story to confirm it.

"But how does it relate to cricket?" Venky mused.

Aki then asked the audience, "Why did Dhritarashtra not stop his son from indulging in his wicked actions?"

A few hands shot up and the answers ranged from 'emotional weakness' to Dhritarashtra himself being evil. Aki then looked at the three monks for an answer and they too couldn't satisfy him. Venky proposed that Dhritarashtra did try to deter his son but not strongly enough. Kishor preferred to remain silent while Shyam spoke about Duryodhana being extremely aggressive which left Dhritarashtra helpless. Aki wasn't impressed and the audience was curious to know the answer. Aki then announced, the correct answer is -Dhritarashtra enjoyed 'extended sense gratification'.

"How many of you wanted to be in the Indian team that won the world cup yesterday? Be honest?" asked Aki. The audience exchanged smiles but no one raised their hands.

"I know you think you are not that good a player; that's all right. But let's be honest, don't we all dream of achieving remarkable success? How many children dream of being Tendulkar and Dhoni and playing the winning shot that wins India the match? How many of you wish to raise your bats in acknowledgment to the 50,000 plus crowd cheering in the stadium? But the truth is only eleven Indians make it into the team and for the rest of the 1.25 billion Indians it's somebody else's victory. But the desire to win and be a champion is strong. So now we identify with those eleven players and see ourselves do what we wished we could do with the bat and the ball. We enjoy great success in cricket when we see someone else succeed in the sport. That's an example of extended sense gratification- you can't enjoy yourself, but when someone else does it, it gives you a kick. Dhritarashtra wanted to be the king so badly, yet due to his blindness he couldn't. And upon seeing his son eye the throne and contrive to get it by hook or crook, Dhritarashtra felt hopeful of his own desires being fulfilled. He could now be the king and enjoy the kingdom through his son.

"We want our children to fulfil our unfulfilled dreams and ambitions. I meet some parents who are determined to make their child a doctor. The child thinks he will be a train driver when he grows up and finds it the most exciting profession. The father however is desperate because he feels he himself couldn't be a doctor but would ensure his son became one. Another parent I met wanted his son to be a great cricket player because he himself as a young boy had aspired to be like Tiger Pataudi, charismatic and heroic who got a beautiful Bollywood damsel as his wife. But this gentleman wasn't that lucky. But he sought to live his secret dream through his son playing for the Indian cricket team. One reason why cricket is a mad passion is because we want to be great players ourselves and we choose to identify with those players who can help us feel heroic. An ordinary looking actor has a superstar status in Indian movies. People worship him and cheer for him and dance when he comes on screen. The need to be a hero is so strong and the desire to enjoy is so deep rooted."

Venky noticed the audience was listening in rapt attention. No one moved. His sleep too had vanished. Meanwhile Lal smiled and Aki looked towards his host and declared, "Lalji, would you like to share that secret of your bump on the head with your friends here?"

Lal began to laugh, "I don't mind if it helps you drive home a point."

Lal and Aki were good friends and had known each other even before connecting at the yoga mission of Swami Abhayananda Tirtha. Aki knew the secret behind Lal's prominent patch of stitches on his forehead above the right eye.

Lal reminisced, "I think I was around eight or nine and wanted to be a great all- rounder like Sir Garfield Sobers. I day-dreamt often, that I'd be hitting six sixers in an over because Garfield was the only one who had done so at that time. He was also the highest scorer and I wanted to beat his record. One early morning as I lay on my bunk bed day dreaming that I was hitting sixers and fours, I slipped and fell on the ground with a loud thud. I had badly hurt my nose and head, and my younger brother who was on the lower bed ran outside and called my parents. I was unconscious and needed stitches on my head."

The guests laughed at Lal's animated description. He loved to crack jokes at himself, and that made him endearing to all.

"So, as I was saying, we dream big and then secretly enjoy others' success," Aki continued his philosophical discourse. "And if our heroes fail, it's devastating because it's 'Me' who has failed. In this dog eat dog competitive world, where even for a small security guard job we have ten thousand applicants, everyone is desperate to feel a strong sense of worth and happiness. And if our heroes fail, it's common to see television sets broken and the best of players are jeered at because they have failed to meet our expectations.

"I dread to imagine what would have happened had India lost the match yesterday."

"Nothing sir, life would have gone on as usual," a middle -aged man sitting relaxed on the family sofa commented loudly, "We would have burnt a few shops, carried the funeral procession of the Indian player's effigy's like we did after they lost the 2003 world cup and then booed them and pelted stones at their houses, and harassed their family members, and finally, life would go on as usual."

Aki acknowledged the comment and continued, "Please consider, why such extreme reactions. Why is there an obsession to win; why identify with the game so much? This is subtle, extended sense gratification which means we enjoy through others' victory.

"It wasn't so bad until a few years ago. We could cheer a Pakistan cricket team and still feel happy about it. We all had different favourites even within one family. You weren't called a traitor if you loved Zaheer Abbas nor were you told to prove your patriotic credentials by booing the Pakistani team. It was a simple sport because life was simple then. Now it's too aggressive; life and sport. What do you say Venkateshwara? He is our, in -house expert on cricket?"

"Really?" Lal's voice was louder than the amplified sound of Aki's speech. "I didn't know you had cricket experts in the monastery? Of course, Venky is now a legend thanks to Maharaj glorifying him the other evening during the YOL festival." All eyes were now on Venky.

Venky spoke, "As a teenager during the 1996 world cup we were in Pune and watching Kenya play West Indies. The stadium was roaring with anti-Pakistan slogans; '*Hai hai* Pakistan' was the common refrain amongst the 25,000 crowd. My friends were tearing their lungs out and while I refused to shout like the others, they ridiculed me for being unpatriotic. That's when I learnt that to show your loyalty to your Nation and the cricket team, you need to hate others and ironically neither India nor Pakistan was playing that match."

"Thanks, Venkateshwara," Aki felt vindicated. And Venky too was delighted to serve Aki by sharing his own example.

"That's madness and not cricket at all." Aki was now loud and emphatic.

Kishor moved closer to Venky and whispered, "He is entering a dreaded zone. You can't criticize cricket in India and get away with it. He's doing exactly that. I have learnt my lessons, and I hope he too learns it soon."

"You are saying that?" Venky looked surprised.

"Yes dear, now I am baptized. I know cricket is not bad. It's the attitude of few crazy men that needs to change that's all."

"Sir, I hate to admit, but you are right," the same man who had earlier commented from his sofa now got up and asked for permission to share his realization. "Please," Aki encouraged him.

"I was at the Wankhede stadium when Sunil Gavaskar played his last international match which was the semi-finals against England during the 1987 world cup. He was booed by his own home crowd as he walked back to the pavilion after a cheap dismissal. India lost that match. I felt sad because Gavaskar at that time was a legend. He had scored the most runs and centuries in international cricket but no one in the packed stadium acknowledged this fact even as the English players lined up and offered a gracious applause of honour. It was a pitiful sight, here in his own Mumbai his achievements were ignored because the crowd wanted to see the Indian team win the match.

"I remember a few years before this incident, a man dying of cancer had approached Gavaskar and had requested him to score a century because that was the last wish he wanted fulfilled before he died. That's how popular Gavaskar was, yet during his last international match, in front of his own home crowd, he was scorned. So tragic isn't it?"

"Hmm…so the point I was making was…" Aki smiled and paused.

"I think I am lost," confessed Aki, "I am sorry, where were we."

"Oh no, please don't be sorry," another guest, a neighbour of Lal spoke up. "We are happy that you are addressing the issue that burns our Nation. In fact, the discussions are so relevant in the current times. I was wondering why Lal called me for a satsang and I couldn't refuse him. But I am so happy I came because you are addressing our issues. This is really important."

"Yes, we were on extended sense gratification, and Dhritarashtra," Aki regained control of the talk, "Let's not forget the theme. We suffer because we enjoy and when we can't enjoy something ourselves, we identify with those who can and then seek the same pleasure subtly in our minds, through their enjoyment."

"But what's wrong with that?" another neighbour was curious to know.

"Oh, we deny ourselves a higher source of pleasure; the pleasure experienced by connecting to our own selves, and to God. We are so lost in the petty pleasures that we forget we have an existence beyond this game. There is more to life, but the gushing waves of the river of time will soon separate us from our positions and possessions. And then we will lie on our deathbeds lamenting at our lost life. Cheer up, be happy in life and seek spiritual pleasures beyond cricket, Bollywood and politics."

More questions followed and an elderly lady, a retired school principal spoke up, "I am glad you discussed this because somebody else plays cricket and earns money and enjoys. We just waste our time and money watching them. I never understood why people spend their precious time on this silly game?"

"Oh, it's definitely better than your silly kitty parties," her husband seated on the other end of the hall shouted while others laughed.

The mood was light and everyone seemed to be enjoying the program.

A lunch feast of *Dhoklas, Oondhyu, Puris* and other traditional Gujarati items followed the event. Venky and Shyam filled their tummies, devouring each delicacy while Aki and Kishor nibbled silently.

❑ ❑ ❑

PART - 2

CHAPTER 2

Shyam's Tryst with Destiny

Lal came to the station to see them off and confessed to Aki, "Thanks a lot; for a long time, I wanted my friends and neighbours to take to spiritual life but didn't know how to connect them. But you spoke exactly what they needed to hear. You are a genius Aki." Aki was modest and thanked his host for inviting them.

The train left the station and no one said anything. It was 3.00 pm now and the coach had more passengers than the morning. Still it was comfortable- if you could say so- because one bench in any compartment would comfortably seat only three passengers but the fourth man would squeeze in with barely a few centimetres of space to park his bottom.

And today it was Shyam who struggled to retain his balance as his left buttock slipped away from the seat. Meanwhile more passengers joined in at the next station. They were standing and the crowd coupled with the noise made their conversations inaudible.

"There is no way we can hear Shyam's story now," Venky reminded the others about the pending story.

At Borivali, many people got off and new passengers entered. As the train halted, almost instantly Shyam and Kishor got up and rushed to the seats in front of Aki and Venky. Now the four were facing each other and a meaningful chat was more likely to take place.

"Yes, our dear Shyam is now going to unravel the mystery of his history." Venky said and moved forward while Aki and Kishor smiled at Shyam, and sat straight.

Shyam began his story, "I was seventeen years old, playing cricket for my school and had set my goals to play for Mumbai first and then India. My hero like other young boys was Sachin Tendulkar and Anil Kumble. We played cricket at the Azad Maidan, a 25 -acre sports ground next to the CST railway station.

"When batting, we'd face the leather ball which is hard and deadly when thrown by a fast bowler. We had a protective gear to cover our head, arms, face and testicles. But while fielding, we had to be more alert because the ground had over twenty cricket pitches and different groups played all over. Suddenly a ball could come crashing down from anywhere and take you by surprise. Our reflexes got really good, and that's why it's said, those who survive the war field of Azad Maidan grow to be really tough cricketers.

"One afternoon as I was fielding close to the pitch, the batsman ran a quick single. The fielder threw the ball at the wicket keeper who in a hurry to dismiss the runner grabbed the ball and instead of merely removing the bails, he pulled off the stumps. So sudden was the pulling that the keeper hit the wickets right into the eye sockets of the rushing batsman. It all happened right in front of me, and in seconds I saw the pitch cascading with blood. Amidst the panic and painful screams, I felt jolted. Hours later I learnt this young boy, a budding cricketer like me had permanently lost both his eyes. The incident shook me.

"That night I couldn't sleep. The next time I came to play at Azad maidan, my stomach recoiled and my heart nervously skipped beats. I wasn't sure if I was doing the right thing. I kept wondering about life; why such accidents happen and why death came so early to so many and what is death after all. This question intrigued me for days while externally I continued with my life as if nothing had happened. I went to the movies, smoked and drank at the local bar with a few friends, and got drunk occasionally but internally I wasn't there. And then another reality hit me. And that was the turning point of my life."

"Oh My God!" Venky exclaimed, "You actually smoked and drank. No one would believe it; you seem to have popped out of the spiritual world; from a world of childlike innocence and spiritual purity, as if these habits were unknown to you. I also can't imagine you were witness to such a ghastly accident."

"For me your playing cricket itself was far out," said Kishor wryly and then he smiled, "I thought I was the only smart one in our ashram who played cricket and had girl-friends and knew the world. But I must confess you have stunned me with this story. Wow! This is far out."

Silence!

Shyam's eyes were moist and for a few moments, no one spoke.

Aki broke it, "What an irony; in this crazy, crowded and noisy Sunday evening local train we are all silent." "I am speechless," Kishor interjected.

"I am sorry I am sharing my own long story, but I have to end with this one," Shyam continued.

"Wait," Venky said, "Oh Kishor, you had girl-friends, uh?"

"Yeah, but …"

"But what?" Venky's eyes beamed, "Guys, I can smell a juicy scoop coming up. Can't wait to hear more of it."

"Who was that unlucky girl you left crying because you wanted to be a monk?"

"Oh, nothing so exciting," Kishor said. He didn't like to be the centre of discussion.

"I am sure all of us want to know more about your adventures with the high- profile glamour girls of Mumbai." Aki said unemotionally.

Venky held Kishor's hand, "You had a steady girl-friend, then why did you leave her, what happened?"

"It must have been love, but it's over now..." Kishor hummed nodding his head and smiling away.

"That was my favourite, *Pretty Woman* soundtrack, a ballad sung by the Swedish Pop duo Roxette," Aki blushed.

"Oh, you too," Venky flustered, "You know these pop songs, I thought you were a born saint who had nothing to do with Pop music and Hollywood."

"Remember every saint has a past and every sinner a future," Aki was now echoing Kishor's buoyant mood.

Venky got up with a start, "You guys are unveiling sensational stories; I am so excited."

Just then a middle- aged man who had been disinterestedly holding the overhead bars with his hands, standing close to the monks like the hundred others in the coach, pounced down on the seat. Feeling comfortable on the seat, he gave out a smile of relief.

"Oh, you lost a seat," Aki laughed at Venky's loss.

"That's ok. I now need to know more of the mystery that you are unravelling."

Aki dismissed with a wave of his left hand, "Remember Venkateshwara, there are many closely guarded secrets in the renounced order."

"I guess that's another of your cryptic clues for something exciting coming up soon."

"Anyways, Shyam what was that reality that hit you, the turning point of your life?" Kishor bought them back to the present.

Shyam inhaled deeply and first sighed. Then he continued, "On 13th March 2003- a hot and busy evening as usual I was returning home with my friend after playing a cricket match at our favourite Maidan. We travelled together seven days a week in the second- class coach of the suburban trains. This particular evening, we had a minor altercation and I was peeved by his behaviour at something that I don't even remember now. As we boarded the coach, I suddenly got down and said I'd rather not travel with him but board the next compartment of the same train. He was already irritated with me and now he got angry and demanded I travel with him. I said no and insisted that we leave each other alone. He pulled me in, while I pushed him away and the curious onlookers saw we were friends but now upset with each other. They smiled at our love-hate exchanges. Meanwhile the train was about to start and I ran away from him and boarded the very next compartment, and assured him we'd meet after we got down at Thane half an hour later.

"As the train rattled along carrying 5000 passengers while it had a capacity of a mere 1500, I hung along near the door. Half an hour of dull moments passed as I got lost in my thoughts...

"Bang…an explosion!

"The train shook violently throwing us off from our positions and the noise deafened us. I thought I saw Mr Death somewhere nearby smile quietly and carry on his business.

"Before I realized what had happened, the train stopped and people panicked and jumped off the train from both sides. Screams and howls added to the confusion. I was numb as a statue and soon learnt it was a bomb blast. But surprisingly I saw no fire or death or mutilated bodies anywhere around. Then slowly it dawned on me that it was the adjacent coach of the same train that had shred to pieces. And then a momentary relief that I was still alive.

"Oh no, my friend! He was in that compartment.

"I jumped off and as others scrambled for safety, I tried to make sense of it, but soon realized I too was disoriented. Is my friend somewhere amidst this huge mass of dead and maimed bodies that were unrecognizable? The agonizing screams of those who lost their limbs scared me but I had no time to feel anything; I was desperate to find my friend. Soon I felt helpless as the crowd swelled, ambulances, police and news channels flocked and I was horror-struck at this bizarre situation.

"I don't know what happened next. I don't remember anything except that I was at the police station a few hours later explaining I had lost my friend. That's where I also met his parents who had come there wailing and confused.

"Soon I was surrounded by a heap of dead bodies, trying to recognize my friend. The nauseating smell and the terrible, shrilled emotions left me desensitized to any feeling. I had no time to cry or feel sad; I had many things to do; to identify him, to pacify his family; to make sense of it all. It was only several days later that I actually broke down.

"And then a constant question hit me; who am I and why was I spared of a sure death that evening? And why did he die? Why bad things happen to good people? My quest to know the truth soon became an obsession. Something and someone beyond all of this world was calling me; beckoning me to abandon my old ways and seek connection with the divine.

"I had known then that six years ago, Raman Lamba, a former world level cricketer died when a cricket ball hit his head. I had never seen him play but heard he was a charismatic player who played well for India. We also spoke sometimes about Nari Contractor, considered as a glamour boy of Indian cricket, a stylish left- handed batsman whose career abruptly ended after a cricket ball hit his skull and he remained unconscious for six days. But I never thought it would happen to me and if we ever spoke about death, it was casually as if it was a foreign phenomenon that happened to others. But after the eye accident, I was shaken and then seeing so many dead bodies after that nerve racking train blast; the whole paradigm of my life changed. I felt I had grown up and wanted to know who I really was and who is God and converse with God, if he ever existed that is, and ask Him all the questions.

"I guess the universe conspires in your favour when you desire something strongly. A month after the train blast I received a flyer advertising a six -session course titled, 'Journey of Self Discovery' and there was Aki, master class presenter. He answered all my questions; does God exist, who am I, the search for happiness, one God or many Gods, why bad things happen to good people, Yoga and practical living, and many more. I was hooked after that.

"I began frequenting the monastery and there I heard others and soon made many friends. It was a gradual and organic transformation of my consciousness. I don't know when and how it happened, but slowly I began to feel that I should dedicate my life to this cause and help others practice yoga, meditation and find their own answers in life. This is a personal and fulfilling journey."

Venky and Kishor looked at each other and smiled while Aki sat gravely.

"Life sobers us up," said Aki.

Venky said, "Oh, we missed our station. It's Marine Lines, and we crossed our station twenty minutes ago. Now our tickets aren't valid anymore."

Hurriedly all four of them got down, and crossed the platform and took a return train. Nervously eyeing the evening crowd, they looked out if a ticket examiner was around. They had erred and if he caught them he would extract a huge fine. Luckily that evening, nothing happened. The four were silently waiting to return and soon they were back at their station.

Once out of the station, Venky heaved a loud sigh of relief. "What was that love story of yours Kishor, we missed it?"

No one answered. Venky realized he shouldn't have asked the question as they were still shaken by Shyam's description of the train bomb blast.

Venky noted that evening the monks who were generally chatty when together, today walked back to the temple slowly and quietly.

The juicy girl-friend secrets of the monks could wait for another day and time. It would be improper to touch that topic now.

❑ ❑ ❑

PART - 2

CHAPTER
3

The Lonely Struggle

"Oh God! See that," Kishor, usually reticent, was now loud. He pointed to Parameshwar, an elderly member of the monastery, eating *Paani puri*, a common Indian street snack, off a roadside stall. "That's our Parameshwar; how could he do that? What would people think? A monk eating outside food like the commoners, this guy is a disgrace to our ashram!"

"Shh...relax," Aki grabbed Kishor's arm, "Just leave him alone, he's an old man. Let him enjoy his quiet snack. Maybe he too is celebrating India's victory."

Others laughed. Aki had the uncanny ability to lighten up when things got heated up in the ashram. And conversely when members were complacent, he'd shake them with his sarcastic and heavy words.

Today he urged the monks to be sensitive to this old monk. "Poor fellow, he has no friends. Most of our monks like you guys are young and restless. He is over sixty- five years old, let's trust him, and leave him alone."

"Does old age make one lonely?" Shyam's question was guarded.

"Hmm..." Aki said, "Let's cross the road over to the beach and sit there for some time. Maybe for a few minutes we can take in the fresh air coming from the Arabian sea."

Seated on the soft sands of the Chowpatty beach, they quietly watched the sunset while around them children played with balloons, couples kissed unabashedly, young boys cracked ribald jokes and families devoured the different street snacks that the Chowpatty beach was famous for. No one gave the group a second glance.

As others sat surrounding Aki, Venky spoke, "Once Parameshwar did tell me that he became a monk by accident. He wished he was married but said that it was too late now and would prefer to quietly struggle here than to leave the ashram."

"Shh.... these are not to be shared with others." Aki mildly reproached the innocent Venky.

"Oh, I am sorry," Venky said, "I realize this is very personal."

Aki said, "It's ok, now all of you please keep this to yourselves. Don't share these things with others as this may confuse the younger inmates of the ashram."

"Yes, old age brings loneliness," declared Aki, "As things around you crumble, you become insecure. And the worst part is if you are successful in this world, then you have many seeking your friendship but you can hardly trust anyone. Then you don't have to wait to get old to feel lonely and depressed. Therefore, monks or others, it's imperative for all to stay focused on their vision and goals and move on in life gratefully and cheerfully.

"Do you know that for all the glamour of cricket, there is a sad, lonely side to it? Players are away from home for days, and must perform. There is pressure from everyone. Most buckle under pressure and get lonely. Similarly, the monks, they have left home, and have to constantly 'perform' for the pleasure of everyone else. Some go bonkers; it's natural to succumb to the mental stress.

"The moment you get some recognition and praise-like many monks do get- you taste the intoxicating effect of worldly glory. You then want more of it. And that affects your basic spiritual practices. We seek external rewards from the world while internally we suffer because we are disconnected from the self."

Urged by Aki, the four of them rose and now quietly walked towards the shore as the waves hit the rocks and many young boys and girls played in the black, foul smelling ocean water.

Venky probed, "I guess then eating *paani puri* from a road side stall is a harmless de-stressor."

Aki said, "Yeah, why make a fuss of it when the poor fellow is saying 'No' to so many things and carrying the huge burden of people's expectations. Younger monks don't realize that as you get older, life too gets tougher. It's like the young Indian cricketers who win the Under 19 world cups. Most of them fade away, and as they grow up, they don't even make it into their state cricket teams. Why is that so?"

Shyam volunteered, "They can't handle the pressure of the game. I mean it's tough. Even young 14 -year old boys carry their huge cricket kit bag and travel from Dahanu to Churchgate, a good 140 kilometres, alone in the crowded local trains, to play a cricket match. They sacrifice their studies and relationships and there are thousands of such boys in Mumbai alone."

Aki said, "Yes Shyam, you know better, you have played serious cricket. I am sure Kishor too has a lot to say on this. You played big time cricket, right?"

"Forget it," Kishor was terse "I was lucky; I didn't have to travel and had my own cricket pitch and coach at home. I mean I didn't struggle at all. I just enjoyed my game but I guess you guys know better because that's what it is for most people."

"Oh yes you are a millionaire's son," Aki smiled, "Oh how easily we forget because here all of us are equals, praying and studying together, sleeping on the same hard wooden floor, eating the same food, sharing our joys and sorrows with minimum wants."

"What about loneliness?" Venky was curious.

"I was not like Kishor," Shyam said, "I played cricket, struggled in life and felt lonely and hurt when I missed the selection for the school team."

"But even those who made it big, they too lost out. Amongst friends, we discussed often about many youngsters like Siddharth Kaul, Ajitesh Argal, Gaurav Jathar, M. Tripathi and others who were part of the world cup winning side as teenagers but succumbed when faced with the realistic challenges at the senior level. When you win the world cup as a young boy, the media goes gaga over it but life has more to it than cricket, and young boys don't realize the tremendous pressure that's coming soon. It's frustrating to handle failures."

Aki spoke, "Success at youth is not easy to sustain as you get older. If you are not grounded, you fly high but end up with swollen heads. The transition from boyhood to manhood is not easy.

"We honour these heroes one day and forget them the next day. Life can be nasty. These are talented young boys; they need to be trained to celebrate life. Let them lead a happy and meaningful life. Not realizing that there's more to life than success or failure on a cricket field, many young boys break down mentally, and are unable to reconcile to the recurring challenges and obstacles in their personal lives. When they are successful they are given monetary rewards, and tempted with more; they are drawn to money than nobler values.

"Beware of success friends!" Aki now raised his pitch, "Bhagavad Gita says tolerate both happiness and distress. It may appear strange, why tolerate success? That's because the temporary fleeting successes of this world have the potential to become a distraction."

Kishor said, "It's getting late, we should go back to the ashram," we didn't sleep last night and now again its 10.00 pm."

Shyam said with beaming eyes, "Yes, Monday morning *Kirtans* are the most exciting and eagerly awaited by all the monks. Let's be fresh and ready for it tomorrow."

Slowly, they trudged back to the ashram and retired. Venky entered in his diary, "Spent a meaningful day with Aki and friends and learnt more about cricket and life."

***

As expected, Venky found the Monday morning *kirtan* ecstatic. While most of the congregation gets busy on a Monday morning with the week's office and work schedules, the temple is quieter and sparsely populated. It's a welcome relief for the monks after the overcrowding experience at the monastery the previous evening. The monks have the temple hall to themselves. They dance wildly and happily. The best singers among the monks usually lead the devotional chants and others sing in chorus and dance rhythmically to the melodies. Usually a new melody is sung the first time during the Monday morning *kirtan*.

"You know it's like Bollywood out here," Aki had once remarked in his Bhagavad Gita class. "It's Friday evening when a new Bollywood movie is released and people are eagerly awaiting the release. The equivalent of that in our ashram is the Monday morning *kirtans*; everyone is eagerly awaiting the release of a new melody."

❑ ❑ ❑

PART - 2

CHAPTER 4

Sachin Retires from Cricket

Days passed and soon weeks and then months. Venky was busy with his youth training services, and stitching monk's clothes; Kishor's day was filled with his outreach programs; Shyam had his temple and ashram maintenance duties, and life went on as usual.

Occasionally Venky would catch Aki and Kishor and wonder aloud about their past lives. Aki simply smiled while Kishor, visibly annoyed, would dismiss it.

One day, Shyam approached Venky excitedly, "Do you know Sachin Tendulkar has declared retirement from cricket? It was an emotional farewell right here at the Wankhede stadium in Mumbai."

"Oh," Venky's expressionless face was misleading. "How do you know this?"

"I had gone to the market to purchase new bulbs and knobs for the ashram bathroom, and there I chanced to hear people speak about Sachin Tendulkar's retirement. Unable to contain my curiosity I asked the shop keeper and he was amused at a saffron clad monk's interest in cricket. He told me whatever he knew and I kept asking and that attracted onlookers. I knew I shouldn't be doing this but I was helplessly dragged by my desire. It was as if a Tsunami of emotions had dragged me away. I have always loved Sachin and wanted to be like him. I felt I was batting when he was on the crease. I celebrated his centuries and mourned his dismissal. I thought what I couldn't accomplish in my life Sachin was doing it for me. And now I couldn't imagine he wouldn't be carrying the burden of the Nation anymore.

"I almost broke down; I haven't missed any of his earlier matches. Before I joined the ashram, I thought God wanted to play cricket and therefore Sachin was born.

"I don't know why but I feel very sad. I haven't seen a cricket match for years but somehow Sachin was India's lifeline. I can't imagine life without him playing for India.

"I was in the monastery but feeling somewhere silently pacified that Sachin was doing well. Now he'd give up cricket after playing at the top international level for twenty -four years. Isn't this awfully painful?"

Venky heard empathically. He didn't speak for a few minutes, and then said, "I share the same emotions."

Both saw several monks walk down the stairs for dinner. The ashram was busy preparing for the evening activities.

Both Venky and Shyam spent some silent moments together. Venky said, "I recall watching Sachin play during the 1996 world cup. I can't imagine eighteen years have gone by in a flash. And I joined the monastery eight years ago and it feels like it was yesterday."

Venky sighed and Shyam too had nothing to say. Kishor was carrying his plate down to the dinner hall and he noticed them.

"Are you guys mourning Sachin's retirement?" Kishor had a twinkle in his eyes as he asked.

"Oh Yes," Venky said casually, "And you seem to know everything we talk and think?"

"I just guessed and since this is the latest excitement in the country, I thought I must share my heartfelt feelings as well. I am remembering Sachin's first Ranji match in 1988, his school matches and then his first series in Pakistan and so many other games he played. I can't believe it's the end of an era."

"Thanks, Kishor for being candid," Venky said, "I appreciate your honesty. I am glad someone else also echoes our sentiments.

"See Aki is coming our way. You think he's aware of Sachin's retirement?"

"If I know him well, he'd be aware but wouldn't care less," Kishor promptly replied.

"Are you guys all right?" Aki hurriedly walked by even as he asked this question. "Tomorrow is my weekly off; I will be spending my day in seclusion without any services or management duties. Would any of you like to join me?"

Shyam and Venky leapt up, "Yes" and Kishor was inexpressive and silent.

"Ok. Be ready at 8.30 am at the temple gate," Aki walked away for his evening services.

The next morning Venky saw over a dozen brahmacharis at the gate.

"What are you all doing here, missing the morning services in the temple?" Venky asked.

"You seem to be restless," Deepak said, "We are all here for the same reason as you. We want to join Aki on his date with Nature."

"But I am sure he wouldn't like it if so many of us accompany him."

Deepak returned the challenge, "Let's wait for him to decide that."

Anxious moments passed. Venky hadn't slept well the previous night, he was excited at this opportunity of spending the entire day with Aki. The last time he had spent the day with him along with Kishor and Shyam had been two and a half years ago when they had gone to the Chowpatty beach in the evening and had seen Parameshwar eat his *Paani puris*.

Now seeing so many monks, Aki may be displeased and avoid going out. Or worse he may prefer to take some other monks with him.

"I don't want to miss this," Shyam whispered to Venky, "and if Aki comes any moment now, he may not take us with him." Another half hour passed. Slowly a few of the waiting monks dispersed away. Others waited patiently.

"I can guess where he could be," Kishor softly told Venky and Shyam. "I searched the whole temple and he's not here. I am sure he's left much earlier today or from the back door. He must have seen a huge crowd waiting for him. I have a strong feeling he's gone to the Mumbai port trust garden. Let's go there quietly without telling anyone. If we find him there, great, otherwise we'll have a nice time ourselves."

The trio excused themselves from the remaining waiting monks and quietly left the ashram premises. They walked briskly to the bus stop and then took a bus further down Mumbai and in forty minutes reached the spacious garden that Aki frequented. Kishor seemed to know the garden well. He had been here with Aki six months ago.

Seated below a pine tree, facing the Arabian sea, Aki was all alone with a paper and pen. Most morning joggers had left the park to resume their daily duties. Only a handful remained, and Aki was busy penning his poems.

"I hate to disturb him," Kishor said.

"What do we do?" Shyam asked.

"I have a suggestion," Venky said, "Let's wait here and chant our prayers softly. Soon he will rise for something or turn around. When he does that he will notice us. And then we can approach him. I too would hate to disturb him now."

Another hour passed. Aki seemed absorbed in his writing. Occasionally he sang aloud. Meanwhile the three patiently waited.

Finally, Aki rose to use the washroom and he saw the trio. Shyam was struggling to remain awake as he repeatedly fell forward, trying to pray on his beads. Venky was listening to Guruji's class on his mobile phone while Kishor sitting up straight was reading from a devotional scripture.

"Oh, what a pleasant surprise," Aki announced. "When did you arrive here?"

Soon the three sat on the adjacent benches and shared Aki's silent and personal moments with the forest. He seemed so much at ease here. He often told Venky that he had a date with Nature once a week.

"Connection comes before contribution." Aki would say and then elaborate further, "If we are living in the external world, being disconnected from our own selves, we can't sustain our services and contribution. We first need to save ourselves; feel loved and nurtured. Only then can we share and serve the world."

These statements Venky had heard in the past, but today it made more sense. The ambience of the tranquil garden and the song of the Cuckoos and even the discordant notes of the crows strangely sounded pleasing.

"You see that Afghan Church," Aki pointed to the imposing Gothic arches across the ocean view. Birds flew over the church and its beautiful stained-glass windows reflected the sunshine.

"Peaceful, isn't it?" Aki asked. As the three of them nodded, Aki said, "Beneath the surface of this peace is deep violence. There is more to life than what you see. The church was built in late 1840's after the disastrous first Anglo-Afghan war where more than 17,000 British and Indian soldiers and camp followers lost their lives fighting against native tribal fighters of Afghanistan. In memory of the thousands who died in the war and the disease that followed, this church was built. Now we come here for peace, what an irony!" Aki laughed mildly.

"And you see this forest. The snakes are always hunting for rodents. The birds for the worms and there is constant fear. Eating, sleeping, mating and defending- these four activities rule the roost in the material world. Even the Afghan war got ugly because the British troops after initial victories had sexual relationships with the Afghan women, and this made the Afghan men furious. It was a direct attack on their 'manhood' that their women had been used by the Britishers. They galvanized forces and eventually forced the British to bite the dust.

"Now almost hundred and seventy years have passed and we come here to find peace. What a place this material world is!"

"You know, I have come to this park before," Kishor said. "I would frequent this with my friends in the early 1990's and it was an open field. The giant trees you see now were all small saplings. The park was conceptualised when I was a teenager. Little did I know then that decades later I would be here seeking spiritual lessons. I can't imagine it's the same garden that I visited twenty years ago. It looks so different."

"Time moves inconspicuously friends." Aki picked on Kishor's lead. "Your finger nails grow, and you don't even realize it until it's time to trim them off. The same with your hair. You don't see them growing but they do and one day you shave off your head because it's hairy."

"Sachin's life is glorious, isn't it?" Venky asked. "I mean we as monks can learn so much from him. To be at the top amongst the world's best and yet remain modest and focused for almost a quarter of a century is no mean achievement. Surely we can learn determination and steadfastness from him."

"Surely", Aki said, "Success spoils even the most talented people. Distractions and temptations are galore in this field. Yet he remained grounded and connected to his family, society and Nation and that is commendable. We as monks don't get even a small fraction of the star status that he gets, yet we forget our purpose and often slip away from our goals. Yet he carried on with amazing attitude. Great man indeed."

Venky grinned broadly, "I feel so happy you are appreciating cricket Aki. I always thought you were cynical about cricket and cricket players. It's so nice that you could see the good in these players."

"Oh, don't count your chickens before they have hatched," Kishor warned, "Knowing Aki, this is not the last you have heard from him on Sachin."

❑ ❑ ❑

PART - 2

CHAPTER 5

Monks Learn from Sachin Tendulkar

"Look at the school kids coming in large numbers. I think it's their school's nature trip." Shyam pointed out to the daily ritual where different schools sent their students as part of their nature study.

As the kids jumped and yelled, their teachers silenced them. Other teenagers from the nearby slums were running on the shore of the ocean. "I too ran on the ocean waters as a young ten -year- old," Aki reminisced. "I want to do that now, but my body won't allow me to. Forty -five years have passed like this." Aki snapped his fingers to indicate an instant. "It's happened so fast."

"Funny how we all look at the watch differently. As young boys, we look at the clock and wonder why it is moving so slow. We want to grow up and have fun and explore the world. We are full of energy and passion. As we get older, we look at the same clock and wonder why it's ticking along so fast. Please slow down; I have many things to do, many plans and desires to fulfil. Please ...but it's too late. Life is already slipping through our fingers."

These impromptu talks of Aki were not unusual for the monks but today it was different. Aki was getting candid. His emotional side was never seen by anyone but today he had entered a different energy field.

Venky later confessed to Kishor that although Aki was deeply philosophical in his analysis of time, yet his child like vulnerability was palpable. It was heartening to see him open up and that too in front of monks who were twenty -five years younger to him. He was a father figure in the ashram, yet here his profound wisdom was the veil that covered his own helplessness.

Kishor asked gravely, "Your career in the ashram is like Sachin's; you have played the 'monk' order for over twenty- five years. What is your biggest realization in life?"

"If it's tough to play cricket at the international level, it's madness to play the 'monk' game for so long. A cricketer has moments when he could chill out with friends and do all that is not cricket. He could also take a break from the game and anyways he doesn't play the game all the time. Moreover, he retires after some years of active play. We on the other hand can't get complacent on our monk duties because the distractions can drag us down terribly, before we know what's happening, we'd slip away from our spiritual standards. There is no break on the path of our spiritual practices and we retire at death. We play our whole life, facing bouncers and googlies and *doosra* and negotiating all the temptations and obstacles. We get injured like the many batsmen who lose concentration and feel the hard ball on their fragile body parts. A moment of inattention in your 'batting' as a monk, and you could hurt yourself badly if not be thrown out of the ashram. You have to constantly be on guard, as the agents of illusion threaten to distract you from your path of submission and servitude to God. So, although we can learn from Sachin but our challenge is greater; our game bigger and our failures magnified but success unnoticed. It's a solitary victory. Unlike Sachin our achievements of selfless service for even fifty years won't be recognized by the media. It's only between you and your Lord. It's for your love of God. That's it.

"This world has no place for you or me or for the timeless spiritual principles. It's busy cheering on the fading stars dancing on the stage of time. While new actors perform on this stage, the older ones are alone nursing their time inflicted wounds, quietly behind the curtains."

Cricket seemed silly now for Venky. He could clearly see Aki and a few other seniors in the ashram, including the sometimes cranky Parameshwar as more glorious than his former hero Sachin Tendulkar. While Sachin indeed was a noble soul, Aki and others faced similar challenges. Ironically while Sachin was hounded by the world, monks were persecuted by their own minds. Sachin didn't let the world affect his batting, a monk too has to ensure that his connection and purity isn't negatively affected by the saffron colour he wears. Venky had heard Kishor tell Shyam at Lal's house a few years ago that the saffron dress was heavy. While a policeman or a doctor or even an army constable would take off his uniform at some time and relax, monks wore their 'uniforms' all the time. They had to bat well, and always. The society expected you to be pure. You lived according to others' expectations and the standards they imposed on the monks.

Aki had more to say on Sachin, "Life could be simple for the monks if they wished to, like cricket could have been a simple and nice game for Sachin if he wanted to. But he allowed others' expectations to get to him. So, we too may succumb to what the world expects of us, and thereby disconnect from who we really are and what we could tangibly contribute to the world."

Venky was surprised, "I thought Sachin Tendulkar always enjoyed his game, and he played naturally and happily, that's why he's so successful."

Aki was prepared for this. "Yes, for most part of his career he was a natural and happy player. But even he went through his struggles and we can learn some valuable lessons from his struggle.

"Initially as a young boy he played cricket aggressively, not being affected by anyone. During the Australian tour of 1991-92, Craig McDermott and Merv Hughes, part of a star studded Australian attack were bought to their knees by Sachin who was just eighteen years old then. The Aussies, well known for sledging, didn't spare this young boy either from their vicious comments. Tendulkar just ignored the sledging and continued hitting boundaries at Sydney, and scored a scintillating 148. McDermott finally challenged him that the next match at Perth, the favourite hunting ground for seamers as the ball bounced hard and high, he would get back at Sachin. But they were shown no mercy even at Perth. Sachin played even better and scored yet another century. He was a young boy then and as Waugh admitted, he toyed with them as if they were school boys.

"But twenty years later when he had ninety- nine centuries in his kitty, the hundredth one became elusive. The media was sensational each time he walked to bat, 'Will he score his hundredth century this time?' The burden of people's expectations was heavy and everyone was asking him only about his 100th century. Even his domestic maid servant was curious to know when he'd achieve this feat. He confessed later that no one spoke about the ninety -nine centuries he had already scored. They were only concerned with his yet to happen, 100th one. He struggled but finally got it against the Bangladesh team more than a year and half later. Ironically, India lost that match. For a man who scored almost five centuries a year, it took him eighteen months to get his 100th one. That's called pressure. As a young man, he played freely; he was in love with the game. As he got older, he carried the burden of desires of millions of people. Although handling pressure can be tricky, to his credit, he survived the ordeal, and came out tougher and more realized.

"As young kids we sing, dance and play with abandon. Soon ambition and responsibilities come our way, and somewhere we forget to enjoy life the way we did as children. Where did that innocent celebration of life disappear? What and whose burden are we carrying in our heads and hearts. Oh, when will I be a child again; oh, when will that day be mine?"

A huge swirling wave rushed to the shore and its sudden splash on the rocks caused it to jump high and far. It kissed the faces of the group that was now oblivious to everything around them. Venky felt the saltiness of the sea water and he could also sense, Aki was emotional.

"I can relate to this so much," Kishor sighed. "I think even monks could be as miserable as others, carrying some unknown burden."

"We all are victims," Aki seemed like an expert in changing his mood. He was now buoyant, and smiled, "The world outside of us takes us away from our true inner self. Like Sachin, we enjoy our spiritual activities during our younger days. But slowly we carry someone else's burden, not knowing what we really want. We get disconnected from our own selves and soon the very activities that once gave us pleasure, begin to choke us just as cricket, the very game that was Sachin's life and soul was now throttling him.

"Although Sachin is a splendid example, not many are as lucky. Katy Sexton, even as a three-year-old child began splashing around in pools and enjoyed swimming. She happily accepted a gruelling schedule and at just fifteen years represented her country, England in world championships. At twenty-two she was a world champion. But soon the pressure to perform got the better of her. She let that affect her. She beat herself up and fell deeper and deeper. She confessed that after training for years, to fall at the last hurdle was gut wrenching. Her internal battles weakened her and she couldn't make it into the National team for the Beijing Olympics. She is now out of the stress, and is more determined to help the society. She offers counselling service to 11-25 -year olds and helps children enjoy their precious lives.

"How reality is far from what is advertised. The spirit of Olympics is 'participation is more important than winning' but that seems like a mere consolation for those who don't win.

"This is the plight of many monks as well."

"Really?" Shyam seemed surprised, "A sacred monastery could also be beset with this kind of pressure?"

"Not all monks," Aki clarified, "But for many, initially we like to practice chanting, hearing, worshipping the Lord and studying scriptures and dancing to kirtans happily. Later as we get older and our 'performances' are noticed, we are appreciated. We are expected to perform better. Each word we say, and the classes we conduct are noted. We are watched. If we forget the essence and get carried away by what the world expects of us, we'd be unnecessarily burdening ourselves. Then we'd not enjoy the simple and happy spiritual process. The simple and natural 'batting' is replaced by a stressful and desperate attempt to perform for others and not for our own purification. It's a pity when a monk becomes a victim of an image that he creates for himself."

"Our spiritual practices are not for worldly glory, just as batting for Sachin and swimming for Katy is not primarily for worldly glory but rather it's a medium of self-expression. It's to be who you are.

"But somewhere tragedy strikes; what the activity can give us becomes more important than the true spirit of the act. If Katy had ignored the worldly pressures and continued to swim and exercise because she loved the sport, she'd be happy and maybe even get more of the external success. Our inner life is the real world. The more connected we are to ourselves the more contended lives we live."

"I think this explains why I am miserable sometimes," Kishor said, "I am sorry to interrupt, but during my initial days in the monastery I was so excited to chant, hear and speak spiritual stuff and I thoroughly enjoyed my life. But now I frequently get irritated. I guess that's because I am no longer performing my spiritual activities as an end in itself but have become selfish, thinking of using them as a currency to get something else in return. Maybe I want appreciation and recognition from others for what I am doing. The same ill afflicts many householders too. They are trapped by the 'have to do' language. 'I want to' is replaced by 'I have to' and that sucks out the juice from their lives. Whether it's the job or family, they are carrying a burden, rather than enjoying it."

Aki laughed mildly while others sat silent. Venky thought there was nothing funny about what Kishor said.

"I am reminded of an incident as a teenager," Aki was now revealing why he had laughed.

"We were highly cricket conscious after India defeated West Indies for the first time during the 1971 series. Gully cricket became common after Sunil Gavaskar's heroics in that series. We wanted to play cricket and become a hero like Gavaskar. One day one of our elderly neighbours, a friend of my grandpa came over to our group and profusely thanked us for playing right in front of his house. We were surprised because in the past he had hurled the choicest of abuses at us and threatened us with dire consequences if we disturbed him with our cricket ruckus. We'd always ignore him, knowing he was a harmless old man. Therefore, it was unusual to see him appreciate our batting and bowling. We felt flattered and happy. He then requested the leader of our group to promise him that he'd ensure we play daily outside his house as long as he was alive. He then called us inside and offered us snacks. We didn't mind that. And as we were leaving he handed us five rupees- a huge amount then-as a token of his appreciation for our excellent cricket.

"We were on a high that evening, we not only enjoyed playing cricket but also got snacks and money for what we loved to do. But we were naïve to the worldly ways; little did we know what lay in store.

"The next day again after our game, he called us in, and showered the same hospitality. This went on for few days. Then slowly he became a little casual and offered only water. One day he was a little rude and we felt like we had been treated like beggars. The next evening, he ignored us totally, and the following morning, he took up cudgels with the leader of our group, who always decided when and where to play. That evening our leader declared to us that this senile old man doesn't deserve to see us play cricket. He doesn't respect us and we shall teach him a lesson by not playing cricket outside his house. What does he think of himself? We are not his servants. We all shared our leader's anger and left his gully angrily, never again to play cricket outside his house.

"Years later when I was in college, the old man died, and his folks had organized a memorial meeting. As his friends and relatives spoke fondly about their memories, I was particularly struck by what his daughter-in-law said. She recalled how years ago, a group of rowdy young boys disturbed his sleep and peace by playing cricket outside their house. I knew she was talking about me and my friends. She then explained how he had been exasperated trying to get rid of us. He then devised a great plan which he confided only to his young daughter-in-law.

"He became loving to this group and pampered their egos by flattery and gracious hospitality. 'That's me' I thought, and the mystery of his good behaviour years ago, got unravelled that evening. He got us hooked to respect. And once we got attached to the admiration we received, more than our game, he played a different card. By insulting us, he hit our egos and to take revenge, we boycotted his courtyard and left elsewhere to play.

"The crowd laughed and clapped at the wily old man's tricks. Some of them pointed to me and we laughed aloud admiring our shrewd uncle from the neighbourhood.

"And again, it was many years later, in the ashram that the spiritual purport of this incident dawned on me. What the old man did is what the world does to us, albeit unintentionally and ingenuously. Initially we pray, chant, glorify the Lord and perform spiritual activities because we want to express ourselves, we want to love and feel loved by God and our own deep inner souls.

"Soon we get recognized for who we are and what we do. Like this oldie, the world appreciates us without any malice. The people who love us are innocent and their appreciation genuine. But we fall for the bait; we take it too seriously and then our practices become a performance. We find the worldly accolades titillating to the senses. Although the reciprocation from the Lord of our hearts is deeply satisfying, the experience is often challenged by various distractions of the world. And then we get addicted to it.

"While appreciation is a good tonic it now becomes an addiction. We can't do without it. We crave for it, fight for it and soon forget the original, pure desire to simply love and chant the holy names of the Lord. The devil of our false ego has got us. Eventually we refuse to practice the sublime spiritual process just because someone has offended us; we sell our souls to the tricks of our mind and egos.

"Human life is precious; we are blessed with the ability to discover rich inner fulfilment through our activities, and bring joy to the lives of others. An Olympic athlete, a movie star or a cricket player may entertain billion plus viewers in over 200 Nations, but should it be at the cost of one's own inner harmony. Could an athlete strive for a gold medal or seek to score a century and be joyful even if he fails? Is the gold chase worth losing the precious diamond of human existence?"

"That's profound," Shyam exclaimed. "Like an expert surgeon, you just dissected the diseased tumour."

"But isn't it natural to seek glory and appreciation from this world?"Shyam probed further, "I mean I do want to become famous and receive love from this world. Isn't it unnatural to deny it?" No one said anything. All eyes were now on Aki.

❑ ❑ ❑

PART - 2

CHAPTER 6

The Magic of 'Visualization'

Aki said, "The bubbling waves on the surface of a river fizzle out in a moment, but the current underneath is serene and steady."

"I don't think I quite get it," said Shyam, "I do feel happy when someone appreciates me and when I am criticized I feel hurt, and angry."

Aki continued, "My dear Shyam, I agree we all need to feel encouraged. But what if we don't get the love and encouragement from others, as often as we wish? Would we stop our pursuits just because no one is appreciating us? On a practical level, an athlete like Katy could translate 'going deeper' in life by asking a simple question: what's the worst that could happen? Nothing really! The burden of expectation is self-imposed. The world doesn't really care whether you win a medal or not. People are busy with their own tale of woes, and if they do criticize you, it's often driven by something negative in their own lives, and has nothing to do with your sporting, corporate or academic performance.

"Realizing that her coveted gold medal isn't going to make a difference to the world could be disappointing to Katy, but it's also liberating. She could now give more than hundred percent to explore the sheer beauty of her performance. She's a great swimmer and she doesn't need the world to endorse it. The accolades are fleeting; our aspirations to harmonize with the divinity within are eternal. Seneca, the great Roman dramatist of the first century, philosophised, 'The great blessings of mankind are within us and within our reach; but we shut our eyes, and like people in the dark, we fall foul upon the very thing we search for, without finding it.'"

Shyam interrupted, "But practically speaking, sometimes I find these things vague. Maybe because I am the youngest in the ashram and haven't seen life and realized deep things like all you people."

"No, no," Aki protested. "Life is simple, and you don't have to complicate it with deep philosophy."

"But I thought that's what you did just now," said Shyam.

"You are offensive now," Kishor curtly stopped Shyam. Venky joined in, "I think you are getting excited and crossing the line."

Shyam quickly apologized and then clarified, "You are talking about all that inner stuff and my basic problem is I can't get even simple things done in the ashram. Like stitching the clothes that the monks give me gets delayed often and that causes me acute stress."

Kishor again raised his eyebrows and this time Aki held his hand.

"No, that's ok," Aki was reassuring, "I see that you want to understand how one could perform better and more joyfully, whether as an athlete, businessman, or as a parent or even as a monk and not get depressed, right?"

Shyam nodded, affirming "Yes, and I am sorry, I got emotional."

"Try the magic of 'visualization'." Aki smiled at the cricket enthusiasts. "Every sports coach teaches his protégés this age- old technique. You can try this even off the sporting field."

"I think you'll need to elaborate," Kishor said and then added, "It's been years since we played cricket and need help to understand in the non-sports context."

Aki was happy to enlighten further. "Before we do anything our mind starts seeing the event. How it will occur and what will be the outcome. This is 'visualization' and we do it all the time. Unfortunately, many visualize a negative result of their task, project, game, or meeting. The negative visualization is also called 'worry', and creating 'worry visuals' in mind often becomes a self-fulfilling prophecy. If you had to walk on a log of wood that's on the ground, it's easy. But if it were placed on a chair it's more difficult and if it was placed in between two buildings, you would imagine falling. However, acrobats would never imagine that. That's how 'visualization' works. You could visualize your performance. How you would treat your employees, how you'd take care of the house, and your behaviour and dealings with your friends. This gives you tremendous confidence when the actual event takes place, because you have already enacted the situation in your mind.

"Having first lived out the event positively in the mind, it's easier to translate it into reality. The pressure is off and the performance smooth. You can take 'visualization' a step higher. Whether you are an athlete or a manager in a company, visualize your life ten years down the line. How would you live your life? Who would be your best friends? What values and principles you'd like to live by? What relationships will really matter to you ten years from now? As you envision the future, ask how much is your present life in line with what you desire to achieve. Will your material achievements, be they a gold medal or a billion dollars help you earn love and peace? Is becoming the most popular and respected person on the planet really worth it? Would you trade your real self for the fleeting promises of this world?

"Remember the Italian saying, 'After the game, the king and the pawn go into the same box.' Keep the visualization realistic. Know that time will invade your bodily and mental faculties. You will not be a sporting hero forever. Ask what really matters to you and are you living your life in accordance with these aspirations. Instead of 'going' through life, seek 'growing' through it. William Stacy, the 18th century American war hero said, 'we should give meaning to life, not wait for life to give us meaning.'"

Äki paused. His eyes were now moist, and with a choking voice said, "I am saying this because I went through a life changing experience myself."

"Tackling challenges in the ashram I remember trying this exercise a few years ago when I was packed with services for over twelve hours a day, and could hardly devote quality time to my spiritual activities. As I felt a growing sense of dissatisfaction despite my busy work schedules, a serious confusion arose in my mind; what am I doing in life? Where am I heading to? I was about to leave the monastery in disgust; the world 'outside' of me had taken a heavy toll of my 'inside'.

"I was saved by Guruji. He asked me to take a break and write down an answer to the question: 'What do I want to be ten years from now?' The answer to this question was candid, notwithstanding my then lifestyle and services. As I envisioned a balanced life of service and worship to the Lord, things became clearer. After the half hour exercise, I compared what I had written with what I had been presently doing in the ashram. The incongruence was obvious and appalling; the train of my life was way off track. It didn't take me long then to come back on track. Since then I have been much more peaceful. Even now I do get lost sometimes but I get the plane of my life back on course. There is a priceless diamond waiting to be earned in solitude and prayer. I remind myself gently, 'Dear Aki, don't let the fleeting gold medals of this world rob you off this diamond.'"

Shyam again interrupted, "And to be honest, I have no time for visualization." He was now cynical.

"You are really pissed because of the errands you run for everybody in the ashram, aren't you?" Venky, his good friend judged the situation immediately.

"No, I don't mind the errands. It's just the ingratitude that I can't take. I do all sort of things like wash clothes of seniors, get food for the sick, rush off to the market for trivial things and then stitch all of their torn clothes. But I feel they just take me for granted."

"All right, all right," Aki took charge again. "I know Shyam, you are really stressed. And besides, South Mumbai is a crazy place, very passionate, with people rushing all around from morning to night. You are a victim of this frenzy. You too have been swept away by Mumbai's cyclonic lifestyle. Why don't you try to slow down?" "And may I know how do I do that?" Shyam asked.

"Hmm let's see," Aki became thoughtful.

❑ ❑ ❑

CHAPTER 7

Aki Teaches 'Slow Down'

"He's going to go off on a tangent again," Venky whispered to Kishor.

"No, I am not," Aki had heard him in the silence of the park.

"See Shyam, our lives are fast, and for no reason. Earlier men played cricket for days together. Then the limited overs match became exciting, and now it's twenty-twenty. Cricket's evolution is indicative of life in general. Life's getting fast both on and off the cricket field."

It was evening now. The sun had almost reached its westward destination. The four of them had walked up to the hillock facing the park and were bidding farewell to the sun.

Aki said, "I was talking to Lalit Parekh last week and he was so stressed out, and wished he wasn't as rich if that meant a happier life."

Kishor asked, "Oh the broker at the Mumbai stock exchange. He is one of the wealthiest in our congregation?"

Aki said, "Yes and he's as busy as our Shyam, earning millions daily with hardly any rest and a terribly deteriorating lipid profile."

Kishor said as a matter of fact, "I heard he recently got another thirty - five hundred square feet mansion at the elite Cuffe Parade for eighty million rupees."

"Yes, and he's as stressed out as our Shyam," Aki winked at the others as Shyam showed irritation. Aki smiled at Shyam, then looked at others, and remarked, "I told him the same thing, relax and slowdown."

"See those parrots," Aki pointed to the birds flying back to their nests on the almond tree. "These birds also live in South Mumbai like Parekh and Shyam, but what a contrast their lifestyle is! While men work hard and suffer, the birds simply exist; they savour each moment and live in the present. The birds' relaxed life reminds me of cricket of the early twentieth century- a bygone age in the history of this game. A cricket match then went on for days and days, and life was pretty much relaxed.

"Do you know about the timeless test of 1939?"

"No," Kishor spoke on behalf of the others.

Aki said, "The South Africans and the English team played a test match for twelve days, and in their first innings, each team scored over five hundred runs. Finally, as the play ended on the twelfth evening, when England, chasing 696 runs needed just forty- five runs to win the match, with five wickets in hand, they realized they had to take a ship back to England. The next morning they could have finished the match in the first hour. But the ship was going now, and there wouldn't be another ship for a few more days. So, they left the match, and what an irony, a match that lasted almost two weeks ended with no result; it was a draw."

"I don't believe it," Venky leapt up, "These guys had nothing better to do?"

Aki said, "Yes that was life then. Just play cricket the entire day, relax in the evening and if nobody won, no one cared."

"And Indians were also good at this. During the first limited overs world cup match in June 1975, England had set India a target of 335 runs in 60 overs, an asking rate of over five runs per over. And guess, how did India respond to the challenge?

"They scored just 132 runs for three wickets with Gavaskar, who carried his bat for the entire innings, remained unbeaten with just 36 runs. It was a notoriously slow and a disgraceful knock, but that was life then. Gavaskar wasn't branded as a National traitor and while the team played more matches and lost most of them, the Indians waited patiently to witness their team win some other match in another tournament."

Venky expressed surprise, "If someone played like this today, he'd be banned from playing the game."

"Yes, that's because we live a fast life, we want everything our way, we are the desperate go getters. We want to win by hook or crook. We want everything at a rapid pace; fast food, speedy cars, reckless entertainment and then a crash! A colossal tragedy!

"Life is not about winning at others' cost. We win when we are gracious in defeat and we lose if we aren't humble in victory. The spirit of the game of life is more important than winning or losing according to the strictures set by the world. I along with my college friends watched India play England in their golden jubilee match in Mumbai in 1980. England was struggling and Bob Taylor was declared out, caught by the wicket keeper. Taylor expressed displeasure at the Umpire's decision and the Indian captain, Gundappa Vishwanath asked Taylor if he had nicked the ball. The English batsman denied and Vishwanath then called him back to play.

"While watching the match at the stands, our group of friends was disappointed at what the Indian captain had done. We wanted to see our team win the match. Bob Taylor then went to play a crucial innings and England won the match. Although we felt sad that India lost, we were also happy to see the spirit of the game. Vishwanath was a tough player and played hard to win, yet there are times when the inner voice, the conscience, tells you what's right and wrong. He did what was the right thing to do even though it cost him the match. He taught us that when we pay heed to our moral compass, we win, even if the world declares us as losers."

"Just see the birds again," Aki urged the group, "And see the men and women rushing in their four wheelers outside. What a gulf of difference, the birds retiring seem to be in sync with nature, isn't it?"

"But we are better off than the animals and birds. They can't enjoy life like we do?" Shyam said.

"Are you sure?" Aki challenged the group. "Can we eat like the elephant, or have sex like the pigeons? It all boils down to eating, sleeping, sex life and defending. The animals can't use their intelligence for anything more than these activities, and funnily, men and women of this world, although they have immense capacity to transcend bodily existence, and experience a higher pleasure, yet they too refuse to think beyond these animalistic activities"

"C'mon Aki, we have the movies, cricket, and the internet", Shyam cut Aki, "Isn't that using our intelligence for a higher pleasure?"

"What does all the enjoyment of this world culminate in?" Aki now challenged more forcefully.

"Sex life?" Venky was sheepish in his soft reply.

Aki nodded in agreement. "Let's admit we are wasting our lives pursuing pleasures that are abundantly available to the animals as well."

Aki's jaw now gutted forward, and his relaxed feet now closed together. He sat crossed legged and straight. He had more to say.

"Such a tremendous potential, but used for mere trifling. Remember a few years ago we gave a couple of hangers to each monk to hang his Kurtas. Soon most of the monks had lost the hangers. No one knew who stole them and when, as these hangers hung our shirts in an open space outside the ashram. It was only months later, while pacing in the terrace of the ashram that I made a startling discovery. I saw on the top branch of a peepal tree a nest made of hangers. When did these birds steal the hangers and how did they learn the art of building nests? Did they study civil engineering? Please know the animals are endowed with intelligence as well. A cat knows when to exactly sneak into the kitchen to get milk. However their intelligence doesn't transcend eating, sleeping, mating and defending.

"Imagine a farmer wins a lottery, and acquires a Ferrari. Would he then replace his tractor with this luxury car to plough his fields? He'd be miserable because the Ferrari is not meant for the Paddy fields. Similarly my dear friends, the animal body and the human body are meant for different purposes. We'd be miserable if we sought the same pleasures that animals instinctively seek. We need to rise beyond."

"And how do we do that?" Kishor looked on quizzically.

Aki said, "Let's begin by being present. Let's learn from these birds and animals the joy of being. Remember we are human being, and not human doing!"

Venky and others shared a prolonged silence. Slowly they rose and walked to the bus stop. They were now retreating to the monastery.

As more than a dozen parrots flew back to their giant residence at the almond, Kadamba, and peepal trees, the gentle leaves rustled at the slightest breeze. Venky looked up at the birds and spoke aloud to no one in particular, "I think this is a beautiful dance. The birds surely have an affluent life in South Mumbai."

"I am remembering Mr Parekh" Aki smiled, "Maybe he could come here and let the trees whisper to him all that he needs to know for peace. Trees are our best friends. The American environmentalist John Muir said it beautifully, 'In every walk with nature, man receives far more than he seeks.' We could learn so much from the flowers, trees, birds and the animals, but to hear their wisdom, our hearts need to be quiet and free from judgement."

❑ ❑ ❑

PART 3
A Love Story

PART - 3

CHAPTER 1

A Secret Wedding

"What the hell is he doing here?" Venky's mind roared and his stupor vanished in an instant. He had risen because his bladder ached; his mind yelled at him to pee.

It was dark and quiet inside the ashram. Even though the streets outside were noisy throughout the day, a deathly silence now pervaded. Inside, it was the monks' snoring that occasionally disturbed Venky but he was now used to it.

He sluggishly walked to the toilet, relieved himself and then trudged back to his bed with drooping eyelids. He saw his watch. It was 1.15 am. He could grab another three hours of rest before the lights in the temple hall- where the monks slept at night- would be switched on. A team of *brahmacharis* would hurriedly wave their brooms to clean the temple premises before it opened at 5.00 am. This spirited event would force the most sleepy-eyed monks to wake up.

On normal occasions, he would hit the hard- wooden floor but tonight, his eyes caught the sight of Kishor outside the gate, seated alone under the street light, next to the almond tree. He was on his mobile phone, absorbed in a conversation and looked intense. Venky's sleep vanished as thoughts gushed through his head, "This unearthly hour, he's all alone there on his phone. That's not him; he's always early to bed and wakes up by 3.30 and is fresh for the morning program. But he looks disturbed now." And that disturbed Venky. He considered going down to meet Kishor to ask him if everything was all right. But he decided otherwise and thought he'd take it up the next morning.

It took him a long time of tossing around on his mat, before he got some more sleep.

"Where is Kishor," Venky asked Shyam during the morning prayers.

Shyam twitched his face to indicate he neither knew nor cared.

Throughout the hour long *kirtans* Venky's eyes searched the hall. He thought of going to Kishor's room and finding out if he was all right. "Let me wait," Venky told himself, but he felt uneasy.

"What could be wrong?"

The *japa* session began; the monks sat in circles and silently chanted on their *tulasi* beads, made of holy basil. Venky leaned over to Shyam a few times and asked softly if he knew the whereabouts of Kishor. Why wasn't he here for his chanting? Shyam's response was the same each time; he raised his shoulder, moved his eyes upwards and shook his head lackadaisically. After half an hour, Venky rose to pace up and down as he chanted. He couldn't concentrate sitting in the confines of a circle.

As he paced in the adjacent hall, he saw through the window, Kishor chanting his mantras outside in the temple courtyard. A few daily visitors came inside the gate while Kishor walking back and forth listlessly, stared at the sky. His fingers hurriedly moved over the beads and his lips gently writhed as if it was a chore that needed to be completed.

Venky reasoned, "I shall wait for the morning class to finish and after breakfast, the first thing I will do is confront him." Venky was used to seeing a more absorbed Kishor during the morning session. It was not only unusual to see him like this but Venky also knew that aimless spiritual activities are unhealthy and for a monk's life, it's suicidal.

Venky then realized it had been this way for the past two to three weeks. Kishor would get up during the chanting, walk away or miss some part of the morning program. It seemed innocuous all the time but after last night's sighting, a certain discomfort and fear seized Venky's heart.

A little later he again looked at Shyam, and wondered if he should share his thoughts with him. But remembering his disinterested response, Venky refrained and looked at the clock. "Just another couple of hours, and then I will catch him."

Just before breakfast Venky called out to Kishor and instantly he looked the other way. "Is everything all right?" Venky further asked and Kishor's one- word answer, "Okay," meant nothing was okay.

"Today's class was great, isn't it?" Venky wanted to break the ice and again Kishor just walked by.

"Can I meet you after breakfast or lunch?"

"I am a little busy," Kishor was abrupt and excused himself. He seemed irritated and Venky thought maybe he wants to be left alone. "Let me catch him in the evening, maybe he'd be a little peaceful then."

He then walked up to Shyam and asked if he could talk to him about something important. Shyam said he was scheduled to repair the *mridanga* in the afternoon and would be sitting behind the *Vyasasan*. "There's nobody there at that time. We can talk peacefully," Shyam said.

Venky knew of Shyam's expertise in repairing temple furniture and musical instruments. The *Mridanga* is a two -sided drum played during the *kirtans*. Shyam also deftly played it with the fingers and palms of his hands. A major part of the monks' Bhakti yoga practices included devotional music and various instruments needed timely attention and repair. And Shyam's favourite place to work was the solitary space behind the *Vyasasan*- a raised seat on which a senior member of the ashram sat while giving his early morning discourse. Later during the day, the upholstered seat stood alone and Shyam found the space between the wall and the *Vyasasan* an ideal place for work, prayers and private meetings.

Around 5.00 pm Venky saw a group of monks laughing aloud in the aisle of the ashram. Shyam was at the centre, entertaining the others. As Venky hurried to the crowd, Shyam exclaimed, clapping his hand on Venky's palms, "You know what I just saw?" Others laughed again.

"I was sitting behind the *Vyasasan*, repairing the *mridanga*, and there was no one in the hall except me. I also had piled up over a dozen kurtas which needed stitches. The temple had just opened for the evening *darshan*. Through the thin gaps I saw a young couple enter the hall and stand nervously in front of the deities. They repeatedly looked around, screening the hall, and I guess they deduced nobody was there. Little did they know I was watching their nervous faces through the designed wooden curves of the seat.

"Convinced there was no one indeed, the young boy picked up his huge plastic bag, opened it and pulled out a heavy rose garland and handed it to the girl. Then he pulled out another one and dropped the bag on the ground. With the decorative wreath in their hands, both surveyed the temple hall, eyeing suspiciously the doors and the windows. Then in an instant, he placed his garland on her neck as she bent low to accept it. Then she put her garland around his neck. Like chickens in a typical village look around fearing a dog or a cat as they busy themselves scratching the soil for insects and seeds, similarly this poor couple was sacred that somebody's going to hunt them down. I sat still, gazing at them, not wanting to miss a single moment.

"He pulled out a steel container from his right pocket, it had red vermilion. Then he gently applied it on the parting of her hair; she was now his wife! From his left pocket he pulled out a cloth, and removed a black necklace strung on a yellow thread."

"I have seen my mother wear it, that's the *mangalsutra*," said Venky.

"And so, it is," Shyam said. "The groom then tied it around the bride's neck and thus the most integral part of the Hindu marriage ceremony was now complete. Both immediately fell on their knees, offered obeisance's to the Lord in the altar, rose quickly, removed their garlands and put it back inside the bag. Then they stood a little away from each other as if nothing had happened moments ago. They closed their eyes and with folded palms, made a desperate supplication; intensely praying for almost ten minutes. I was in splits; it was an instant Hindu marriage; amazing and no one knew about it except the merciful Lord and a snoopy monk, who saw a wedding after many years.

"Slowly other people came in for their temple rituals and for the auspicious sighting of the deities. Meanwhile the newly married couple opened their eyes, and slowly walked towards the exit. I too left my *mridanga* and walked to the door where we hand out a little Prasad to the guests as they leave the temple hall. I now saw them closely; their eyes weren't beaming with the joy of a sacred bonding. Rather it was a relieved visage that acknowledged my greetings. I smiled and handed them each a little coconut sweet ball. But my mischievous instinct got the better of me. I looked straight into their eyes and impassively said, 'Congratulations on your marriage. The Lord's blessings are surely with you.' You should have seen that sight."

Again, a loud laughter attracted more monks and they nudged forward to be part of this entertainment. Shyam was in his elements, "The couple was shocked. I saw their lower jaws drop, and then they immediately composed themselves, slipping a nervous smile and a half-hearted thank you, they fled."

Amidst the loud laughter, one of the monks commented on how young couples falling in love are desperate to get married secretly when their conservative parents oppose the match. They are influenced by the Bollywood movies that script out one romantic saga after another. Then another said something about the Bollywood movies, someone else interjected with his wisdom on what ails the youth of the country. And so, it went on.

Venky held Shyam's hand and pulled him aside as others were now lost in their own gossip world.

"You know something is not funny in the ashram right now?"

❑ ❑ ❑

PART - 3

CHAPTER
2

The Mysterious Kishor and Aki

The three of them were seated in a closed six by six-foot room, with barely enough space for one person to sleep. They could hear each other's breath in the silence. Aki's room was a rickety makeshift adjustment made by the ashram leaders as the number of monks grew, while the premises didn't expand correspondingly. The walls were crumbling and the door was a thin cardboard sheet that would collapse if one of them sneezed loudly. Being a senior leader Aki was offered better facilities to stay but he had refused saying that he was happy and was receiving a lot more than what he desired or ever deserved. His humility was most endearing to the monks and given his immense scholarship and wisdom, for him to be non-assuming and simple in his lifestyle inspired the juniors in the ashram.

Today however Aki had no wisdom to offer. He was quiet and meditative. Gently wiping an odd tear from his left eye, he heaved a big sigh; his eyes were moist, and he struggled to hold back his tears.

Venky had just explained animatedly his concerns about Kishor's mysterious behaviour and Shyam who had dutifully accompanied his friend sat expressionless.

Venky was loud, "Why is he growing a beard? Monks are generally clean shaven! Something's really wrong; he's out of place. I have never seen him in all these years with unkempt hair and long beard."

Aki looked at Shyam who returned the glance and then turned to Venky.

Venky continued, "He's always advocated the need for the *brahmacharis* to go on a retreat", Venky said. "He's been talking about this for years and at last now we have the Karjat farm retreat planned. Everything is ready, and even the monks from our other centres are coming. And now Kishor's acting funny; he's not interested. We even announced we'll be playing a mega cricket match one of the days. I insisted he come for at least two out of the four days, and he's totally indifferent. I told him he would be the cricket captain of one of the teams and while everyone in the ashram is excited to see him play, he's playing truant. I am shocked because he never throws tantrums; he's not part of this ashram anymore."

Venkys' voice trailed off. He then repeated what he had just said and then jumbled incoherently. Aki was patient and a little later Venky paused, apologized and fell silent.

"It's all right!" Shyam said, "You are excited and concerned for a dear friend."

"Even I share the same worries," Shyam now looked at Aki, "A couple of days ago he came to the store room and asked me about my well-being. When I said I am all right and then asked about his welfare, he remained mum. He then said, 'you are young and new in the ashram, Shyam, it's not too late for you to go home. Life is tough out here. Life could get lonely here.' He then walked away. He looked sad and was all by himself."

"So, what should we do now?" Venky asked helplessly.

"Let's hope for the best" Aki said softly and spread both his hands to gently massage the palms of Venky and Shyam. "I wish I had answers, but I am clueless and myself in pain."

Venky and Shyam sat silently as Aki wiped his own tears and put up a brave smile.

Both rose to leave; the door crackled as they carefully pulled it.

Outside Venky turned to Shyam, "I had gone to Aki to resolve one big mystery of Kishor. Now I am returning back with two unsolved mysteries. The most unemotional person I have ever known is Aki and did you notice, he's also crying.

***

Paum.......paum........the horns deafened all. It was 5.00 am. A few neighbours came up to their windows to see who the hell was honking so loud and long.

Brahmacharis seated inside the fifty -five- seater luxury bus felt embarrassed at attracting attention and drawing curses from the sleeping neighbours. But they couldn't help it.

Everyone was ready and excited to leave for the four- day picnic. Suddenly Venky announced that Kishor hadn't come. For the last half hour, a few monks frantically looked everywhere, while the others in the bus got impatient. The exasperated driver honked.

"Shh...It's disturbing. People are sleeping out there." Venky appealed to the driver.

"Lets' leave without Kishor," someone shouted from the back.

Gopal, one of the seniors in the ashram raised his voice, "Don't be so selfish. It's Kishor who's always championed the cause of a picnic and now we want to abandon him. That's not even being decent. And please give Shyam a few more minutes. He has promised he will find and get Kishor to be with us."

"Look, they are coming," a monk yelled.

Venky saw Shyam walk triumphantly as Kishor trailed behind with his heavy bag.

As the bus left the premises, the monks roared in unison. They were expecting four days of fun, feasting, swimming, mountaineering, and lively discussions on various aspects of a renounced life. And of course, a cricket match was also planned!

"Just see, his body is here but he's really not here," Venky told Shyam pointing at Kishor who sat in the last row of the bus. Kishor was staring outside.

"His face has lost its glow. Once upon a time he was so radiant and energetic. What's happened to him?"

"The lustre has weaned away eh?" Shyam said in his biting best, "Lust gets your lustre."

"This doesn't disturb me as much as that," Venky now pointed towards Aki who nodded his head while talking on his mobile phone.

"I am surprised because I believed Aki never liked to talk on a mobile phone, yet here he is engrossed in a conversation, and oblivious to all of us. Something big is cooking up. I hope our party doesn't get spoiled."

"*Arre* just leave it, let's chant our prayers and why speculate?" Shyam seemed to realize that it was none of their business to know what was going on.

The bus drive to Karjat appeared to be uneventful with monks chatting loudly and excitedly with each other. They were catching up with news of the monastery and were also eager to know more about the upcoming retreat.

Venky constantly stole glances at both Kishor and Aki. He saw Aki and Gopal discuss softly. They had serious expressions. "What could possibly be wrong?"

"Stop the bus," Gopal announced.

As the bus came to a screeching halt, Gopal rushed to the front of the bus and announced, "Due to some serious and unavoidable circumstances Aki has to leave us."

"Nooooo..." A few exclaimed in unison.

"The retreat hasn't even begun, and it's no fun without Aki," said one monk.

"He'll join us but a little later. We shall start our program without him. We need someone to volunteer to go with him."

"Who would want to miss the retreat?" Venky softly asked Shyam and just then a loud, 'Me' reverberated inside the bus.

It was Kishor. "I shall go with him."

Before Gopal or Venky could react, Kishor got off the bus with his bag. Aki descended slowly, and the bus sped off.

"That was an anti-climax," Shyam said to Venky. "I tried so hard to get him. I first went to his room, woke him up and then packed his bags. He kept saying his coming to the picnic would be a waste of time. I literally forced him to come, and now he's gone back. Moral of the story- never force a monk to do something. He will just do what he wants to and not what you convince him to do."

❑ ❑ ❑

PART - 3

CHAPTER
3

The Picnic Lesson: 'Be Positive'

"The cricket match will be a damp squib without him." Venky said.

Shyam agreed, "Yeah I heard he was to be the captain of one team and I'd captain another. Since both of us have played professional cricket, the retreat organizers had told us the match would be exciting if both of us played opposite each other. Now all that seems to be over."

"But I wonder what's really wrong here." Venky couldn't get over the fact that Aki and Kishor were missing. "There's something deeply unusual about them."

The Karjat farm was a spacious hundred- acre retreat centre that belonged to Mr Khanna, a Delhi based businessman who now stayed in Pune. He made good money from the farm which he used as a retreat where holiday crowds and corporates used his rooms and facilities for vacationing. Recently Mr Khanna, a devout fan of Guruji and Aki, had requested the monastery to avail of his facility free of cost. He wanted to serve the monks who he believed were so sincere that they selflessly served the world but possessed nothing. In fact, they didn't even take any holidays, and this inspired Mr. Khanna to convince Gopal and Aki- the presidents of the Monastery- to take the monks out on a holiday with all expenses borne by Mr. Khanna. It was too good to be true. Both of them thought a holiday would do no harm, and gave a go- ahead signal.

The next tier of ashram management team then executed the plan. And so here they were, over hundred fifty monks from Maharashtra, on a four- day holiday. The rooms were spacious and the retreat centre included everything the monks wanted, including a decent cricket ground with an amateurish pitch on which one could play tennis ball cricket.

No sooner the monks alighted from the bus, some of them began running and shouting happily. "It's as if these guys have been released from the prison," Shyam mockingly pointed to Venky.

"You are now being as sarcastic as Kishor," Venky said.

Shyam said, "I am in no mood to go for the inaugural lecture. But I guess at least this one I'll attend and then I will wander off to the forest. I am a free bird."

***

"Monastic life is serious business. It's a life of hardships. We have to constantly say 'No' to so many things." Gopal's inaugural lecture was fiery.

Seated at the very end, Venky turned to Shyam, "It's not the same without them. I wish they come and I wonder what's happening."

Venky cautiously raised his hand, knowing well that he'd be disturbing the flow of the talk, "Can you please tell us why Aki isn't joining us?"

Gopal said, "Srinivas has been diagnosed with an advanced stage of cancer. Doctors say he won't live longer than a few days. We have been aware of this since the last four months but the reality is hitting us only now. Aki is disturbed as they are close friends."

"But I have never seen Srinivas and who is he? We live with Aki and how come many of us don't know his close friend?" Shyam asked.

"Oh, I am sorry," Gopal continued, "Srinivas and Aki joined the monastery together way back in the early 1980's. They served as a team on many projects and were happy like all of you are. We were all good friends. One day, Srinivas decided to leave the monastery.

"He preferred to get married rather than endure the hardships of a lonely monastic life. Then he got busy outside getting a job, then a house. Meanwhile we lost touch and met only rarely in some community festival. But our hearts beat for each other. And then we heard Srinivas was in love with a woman. He said he had found his soul mate. They got married and he then started a business. A few years later they had a child and his business stabilized. The cancer news has come as a sudden shock. The last six months has been tough for many of us. We didn't share this news with you because none of you know him. Just the five-six of us who joined way back in the 1980's know him. But yes, Aki is affected and so am I.

"Since the doctors have declared that any day now could be his last, a few of his old friends have decided to be at his bedside. Since Aki even helped Srinivas get married to the girl he loved, he's the most affected. He's doing his best to serve and care at this hour."

After a few moments of uncertainty, Gopal asked, "Shall we continue our class now?"

"Monkhood is the best possible life. No anxieties but only service to God and humanity. It's a simple life, you sleep on the ground, eat the simple food except on special occasions like this retreat, and we carry no money but service as our possession."

"But then why do monks leave the ashram sometimes?" A young monk from the Pune centre asked.

"That's because sociologically it's an abnormal life. Spiritually it's glorious but to live without a companion is artificial, unless of course you are strongly fixed on a transcendental plane. Some realize after a few years in the ashram that they'd be better off serving outside. And it's not a failure if you leave the ashram. The training here for as long as they stay, is only an asset that helps them as they graduate to the householder ashram."

"But we see some older monks get cranky and irritable!" Venky stated.

Gopal said, "As we get older, we have to be careful not to allow any negative thoughts to overwhelm us. We are obsessed with the 'No's' so much that we ignore the positive possibilities in the monastery. Even people staying outside, they get trapped by the thinking addiction. Constantly worrying about their finances, home, partner, family, they fail to live in the present moment. They trade the simple pleasures of life for some imaginary worries. And that makes them irritable."

"But aren't the *brahmacharis* worries of loneliness and lack of security in old age a harsh reality of monk life?" Venky braved to ask this.

He was thinking of Parameshwar whom he had often seen at the beach eating roadside savouries and wandering off mysteriously away from the ashram at early hours on some days.

Gopal now raised his voice, "It may be a reality but do we have a choice? We have to be hopeful. It's our subconscious mind that makes or breaks us. Externally and even internally we may psyche ourselves to believe that we are focused and strong in our spiritual practices. But the subconscious mind which stores over sixty percent of all our impressions and desires runs the show. And most often we are not even aware of it. So, if we add positive thoughts always, then slowly this piles up and shows up on the conscious awareness level as well. A monk therefore has no choice but to improve his mental hygiene by absorbing the positive."

Gopal paused, slipped into a smile and said, "Since we are going to play cricket soon, a cricket example may make sense. Two batsmen play the same shots, they are equally good, and they carefully survey the players of the opposite team, see the gaps in the fielding positions, and then hit the ball hard. Yet one of them hits the ball straight to the waiting fielder while the other steals runs easily through the gaps. Has anyone wondered why this happens?

"That's because although both are determined to score runs, and both carefully study the opposite team, it's their subconscious mind that does the trick. One of them tells a negative story to himself, 'Oh these are the players standing here. I have to 'not' hit the ball towards them but towards the gaps'. Little does he realize, he attracts the same situation that he dreads; he hits the ball in the direction of precisely those places where he doesn't want to. The other batsman also sees the same fielders stationed at critical spots but his subconscious mind takes in the gaps. He has a positive story to tell himself, 'hit the ball right there, in the gaps'. He sees the obstacles, but his inner world has taken the opportunities-the gaps-within this challenge.

"Similarly, my dear friends this principle applies to all; monks as well humans outside the monastery. What you choose to think and take in is what comes out of you. If a person has a negative story to tell himself, the monastery would one day become a dreadful place. And if you are a householder, your wife or husband would constantly make your life miserable if you are always ranting a bad story to yourself. Little wonder then that the older monks too get cranky. We have to help them overcome their loneliness and become positively engaged in their spiritual services.

"This may surprise you but the truth is married people are as lonely as monks. Because loneliness is not dependent on whether you are alone or you have a companion. That's all external. What really determines loneliness is your diatribe within. If a monk thinks 'Oh how I wish I had a wife who would give me love and companionship', that very thought increases his loneliness. Sounds ironical to you, but the truth is, the more we base our happiness on the existence of a past or future event the more the present loses its charm. We start dreading the present because we are busy imagining some future happiness. Then we begin to find the 'now' all the more inadequate and even terrible.

"The reality however is, our loneliness is a choice. Often when we are busy and absorbed in some activity that we love to do, we don't' feel lonely. But when we do feel lonely, it's because we tell stories to ourselves and then we find a vacuum in the present moment. The very hope of future happiness then makes the present hopeless. We are miserable in the present and want to leave the ashram because 'there is no happiness here'. However, the reality is, there is no happiness there either; whatever bliss exists, it's here and now."

A spontaneous applause greeted this profound wisdom of Gopal. Venky later confessed that he thought Gopal is so wise because he's seen many summers and winters here in the ashram. "He's from 'the school of hard knocks'" Venky often told his friends in the ashram.

Gopal continued, "And just one more thing." Even though the applause hadn't subsided, Gopal had more to say, "We have difficulty dealing with this one mind of ours. And then to quell its tirade we get married and then we have to deal with two minds. To escape suffering caused by this duo, we think we'll have kids and then you have one or two children. Now you have four minds to deal with. A monk just has one rascal mind to contend with."

Now loud laughter blended with the applause. Venky realized, "Yes the retreat is on. The monks are on fire. They are happy and excited."

Venky asked Shyam, "But where is Kishor. Will he return? Maybe he's feeling lonely in the ashram?" As these thoughts raced through his mind, the lunch break was announced.

Shyam assured Venky and others, "Gopal spoke to them and assured me they'd be here before the cricket match."

❑ ❑ ❑

PART - 3

CHAPTER 4

The Secret Phone Calls

Venky ran towards Shyam, eyes beaming, "The teams are announced, and you were right."

The swimming pool was packed with the monks in their towels. Some wore shorts and they were shouting, playing and laughing. A loud cheer acknowledged the announcement of Shyam and Kishor as captains of the two teams. The teams were called Krishna and Balram. They would play a twenty over match the next afternoon, an hour after lunch. All were invited to cheer the teams and enjoy a game of cricket.

Venky said, "I just hope the captain of Balram team arrives before the match starts."

The evening *kirtan* session promised to be soul lifting. The best singers and musicians amongst the monks would perform for over five hours. The monks readied themselves for the candle light kirtans under the moonlit sky. In another section of the farm, on the verdant lawns Venky approached Gopal.

"Can you please tell me more about Srinivas. I am saddened to hear that he's dying and Aki's soft side was unknown to me."

Gopal narrated Srinivas's struggles in the ashram and the fun they had while he was a monk.

"Aki would walk in haughtily and throw his shirt at Sinu, as Srinivas was popularly called. He was an expert in sewing clothes and stitching the torn ones. He ran errands, more like our Shyam and was the most loved and non-controversial *brahmachari* in the ashram. The next day, again Aki would bully him about his shirt and demand why it wasn't ready. A bundle of clothes would pile up at Sinu's table and he would happily serve all. Although the service wasn't obligatory, Srinivas just loved to extend himself for others and we took him for granted. We pulled his leg, but loved him. He was also happy until the day he fell in love."

"Oh, I thought he fell in love and got married many years after he left the ashram," Venky said recalling Gopal's morning class.

"That's right but he left the ashram in the first place because he fell in love with a woman from our congregation. She too promised to marry him if he left the ashram."

"Then why didn't he marry her?" Venky asked.

One of the organizers rushed to inform Gopal, "The *kirtan* team is ready and the monks have also arrived. We are waiting for you."Seeing Venky's expectant eyes, Gopal said to the organizer, "You start the program; we'll join soon."

Gopal continued as Venky was in rapt attention, "Her father was furious. He thought a monk had conned his daughter and said he could marry her only over his dead body. The couple's plan was squashed and she didn't want to elope. He was shattered and I was ready to take him back in the ashram's fold but he realized it was foolish of him to return to the monastery. He was not cut out for this. He was used to stitching clothes and now it took him three years to stitch together his torn heart. At last the senior congregation leaders arranged for a nice girl to marry him and what happened after that you already know.

***

The *kirtans* began on a soft, soothing note. One monk played a flute that he had learnt in the ashram during his spare hours. Another played the violin while Shyam skilfully thumped the *mridanga*. Soon the kirtans turned loud and exciting. The monks got up and began dancing, at first slowly, moving their hands and legs rhythmically to the *kirtan* beats and then in circles holding each other's hands. Then as the *kirtan* reached a crescendo, they jumped high and ran and swung in all directions.

"This is the real feast for the soul." Venky said, panting and sweating.

"But look at Kishor, he's over there, far away from all this nectar," Shyam said.

"At least I am happy he and Aki have come back," Venky said.

"Yeah, but he's busy texting. He's always on his phone."

Venky sighed, "These smart phones have destroyed the moderns, and the monks too are victims of this. I just hope he's not in love with some woman."

The kirtan session was followed by a super feast of *Bhel puri, Paani puri* and *Pav bhaji* - popular Mumbai snacks.

Parameshwar looked happy. He winked at Venky, "You won't see me eat this stuff at the beaches again if we are served these in the monastery also, at least once a week."

Venky looked for Kishor and found him outside his room alone, busily texting messages on his I-phone. A monk wouldn't normally possess a mobile leave alone an Apple gadget. Kishor's father was wealthy, and he had gifted his son a phone because he was cultivating prosperous families residing in South Mumbai. He needed an I-phone for his services. And no one in the ashram objected.

Kishor's disinterest in the feast was saddening to Venky. "You are the odd man out," Shyam said to Kishor.

"You should eat something. Is something wrong with you?" Venky probed.

"No…err. I mean I am ok. Some other time, I shall tell you. Please leave me alone for now." Kishor's distraught face evoked compassion in Venky's heart. They both left to honour the feast and they did it justice. Both even made up for Kishor relinquishing his dinner.

***

The next morning's chanting session was in an open garden, under the pinkish hue of the rising sun.

"I don't remember seeing a rising sun in decades," sighed Aki and Gopal affirmed.

Venky who was sitting close by heard them talk while the monks felt that the chanting today had been a refreshing experience.

Aki again broke the silence and whispered to Gopal, "Usually the indoors of the ashram alienates us so much from the rest of the world that a sunrise is a rare delight. What a pity. We need to change the structure of our ashram's lifestyle or else we'll lose more monks."

Venky pretended to be absorbed in his own chanting with his eyes closed, while he tried to catch every word the two senior leaders of the ashram spoke.

The morning dew from the trees fell on the grass and the leaves swirled to the placid wind.

"When is he leaving anyway?" Gopal asked.

"I don't know." Aki shook his head as they continued to softly chant on their beads.

"Who's leaving and when and why?" Venky's mind raced, "Is it Kishor and oh no, we have to stop him from leaving the monastery."

Venky waited for some time to see if the senior leaders had more management issues to discuss. Seeing nothing more come up, he got up slowly, and went searching for Shyam. He had to tell him what he had just heard. And Kishor as expected was nowhere to be seen. Maybe he's not interested in ashram life anymore.

"Huh..huh…auf…" Shyam grabbed Venky with his right hand, held his own stomach with the other and wrenched his face. He just ran a good two hundred meters to catch up with Venky.

Venky said, "I have been looking for you all over and here you are. Gopal and Aki were talking about someone leaving the ashram."

"And that someone is Kishor, he's on his way out, anytime." Shyam declared.

"Are you sure?"

"Yes, I had gone to his room to summon him for the morning session. As I gently knocked on the door and opened it. I saw no one there. I could hear the sound of the toilet flush. I guessed Kishor must be inside and decided to wait. As I casually glanced around the room, my eyes fell on his I-phone. Curious, I checked his phone calls. The logs showed over a dozen phone conversations with Smita and most of them had lasted for over an hour. And one call last night had lasted over three hours."

Venky said, "I wonder who this Smita is? Maybe she's the one luring him to leave us. She's taken a heavy toll on his spiritual health. Poor Kishor, what has happened of him?"

"I then saw his WhatsApp messages. Saw her display picture. She is beautiful! But his chats were not clear as he had deleted most of them.

"I then tried to make sense of them and just then the bathroom door opened and Kishor came out and immediately he was alarmed at my presence in the room. He rushed towards his phone which I had flung on his bed. While pretending to talk to me, he checked his phone and I could sense he was erasing more evidence."

"Hmm... this is serious," Venky said. "A monk is not supposed to have intimate associations with women, and I fear Kishor has just crossed the line."

During the morning class Aki had spoken from the Srimad Bhagavatam and narrated the episode of Ajamila dying while chanting the holy names of God. There was no humour in the class. Venky guessed Srinivas's cancer was still ringing heavily in his heart.

Slowly Venky rose and walked behind to where Kishor sat. He smiled at Kishor, who moved his head just slightly to acknowledge Venky.

Kishor seemed spaced out and distracted.

"Can I borrow your phone for a moment?" Venky asked.

Venky had planned to ask this question to catch Kishor by surprise. But Kishor seemed prepared. He handed over the gadget to Venky without the slightest hesitation and continued staring at the vast expanse of fields and mountains facing the farm.

After a few moments of fidgeting with it, Venky returned the phone. "It's off. Please switch it on."

Kishor casually put it back in his pocket. "It's discharged and there is no electricity since morning."

Soon the class got over and Aki announced there would be a cricket match in three hours from now and Shyam and Kishor would lead the teams.

A loud roar greeted the news and suddenly all eyes were on Kishor.

"I am not playing any cricket," Kishor protested feebly to Venky.

"It's too late sir. We are dying to see you bat. We've heard you are graceful like V.V.S. Lakshman."

"Sorry, I wish you all the best," Kishor was assertive and then his voice boomed. "I am not playing and none of you can force me."

He then pushed Venky and shouted into the air, "I am done with this. I quit."

As Kishor stormed out of the assembly, a stunned silence gripped the group. Seconds earlier there had been a celebration and now a hushed calm prevailed.

❑ ❑ ❑

PART - 3

CHAPTER 5

The Cricket Match

The lunch's main attraction was the dessert- mango ice-cream. For many monks, it had been years since they had eaten an ice-cream.

"This ice-cream wouldn't cool down Kishor. It's getting really hot for him," Shyam told Venky during the meal.

Venky comforted the monks, "I heard Gopal reassure Aki that he'd spend time with Kishor and reason with him. He promised me he'd get him to play the match."

The fluorescent yellow tennis balls teamed with the bright orange robes of the monks looked amusing. Venky was fascinated to see the twenty-two monks play on the grassy field of the farm which was around 350 feet in diameter, definitely shorter than a professional cricket field.

"That's all right," Aki remarked about the field, "For the tennis balls which are much lighter than a leather cricket ball, the ground is perfect. Our monks can hit hard and can score boundaries easily on this ground." He winked as he rushed to the field.

They had pulled up their *dhotis*, flexed their muscles and clapped their thighs and biceps indicating they were ready for the clash of the titans.

"How did you manage to convince him?" Venky asked Gopal as they took their fielding positions on the sandy ground. It was dusty, and hot. However, no one objected. The sheer pleasure of getting to once again wield the bat and throw the ball and relive the pre- monk days seemed liberating.

"Not now, we will talk after the match. This is a serious game, we have to win." Gopal ran to his fielding position and the monks laughed to see Aki swing his bat.

Kishor had won the toss and elected to bat. He opened the innings along with Aki.

Venky noticed Kishor was a different man. He was all smiles and also in a trance like state. He seemed so natural swinging his bat.

Venky, who preferred to keep wickets, told a friend at the slips, "The saffron robes are surely heavy on him but a cricket bat in his hands gives him such a divine look. He's so natural. It appears he was born with a cricket bat in one hand and with a silver spoon in the other."

The innings was a delight to watch. As the monks struggled to bowl a straight line, Kishor effortlessly danced down the pitch and hit the ball for sixes. He drove through the covers gracefully. It was a perfectly choreographed tango- abruptly he'd hit the ball hard while he gracefully ran between the wickets. The loud cheering from the stands was the perfect music accompanying his performance.

Venky, the wicket keeper roared, "What a scintillating shot, wow! A sheer beauty to behold." He was glad he was keeping the wickets, as he could watch Kishor bat up - close.

As the monks cheered him on, Kishor raced up to his fifty by the ninth over while wickets on the other end fell rather in a clumsy way.

One batsman swished the bat, missed the ball and lost his balance and fell on the wickets much to the amusement of everyone. Another, in an attempt to steal a cheeky single, ran straight to the umpire and hit him hard and both of them fell on the ground. The crowd was in splits when the elderly Parameshwar ran fast for a third run, and his *dhoti* fell off. But undaunted he completed the run in his loin cloth. He even waved his bat to the audience to acknowledge their cheers at every run he scored.

When Kishor was on the crease, it was different. Shyam bowled straight length, the ball swung, yet Kishor's square cuts bought loud cheers from all. He was all concentration but seemed to also enjoy the attention he got. He played the leg glance, square drive, pull, hook and cross batted sweep to its precision. During the fifteenth over, a huge crowd of monks rushed en masse to the pitch to congratulate Kishor. He had hit a huge six, his seventh one and scored a century. Already two balls were lost in the thorny bushes beyond the fence. Fortunately, the organizers had bought a dozen tennis balls for the match.

By the middle of the sixteenth over, Balram's team was all out. Yet the umpires allowed more batsmen to come and join Kishor. It was mandatory for the team to complete twenty overs of batting even if over two dozen batsmen were dismissed in the process. At the end, team Balram had totalled 177 runs for fifteen wickets with Kishor unbeaten at 121.

"Just look at his broad smile, open chest and outstretched arms," said Venky, "He's liberated from the shackles of issues bothering him. He's attained nirvana."

Venky congratulated Kishor, "I dropped a few catches but you were flawless. You look so blissful. You have surely missed this the last eighteen years."

Kishor simply smiled. He had nothing to say. He savoured each moment of the attention and praise he received. He gratefully acknowledged all pats on the back and words of appreciation.

"But now the innings is over, yet you refuse to give up the bat," Venky chided jokingly.

Shyam turned to Venky, "He's a transformed man. Who would believe he's the same depressed Kishor who's not happy in the ashram?"

Team Krishna began their chase cautiously. Venky and Shyam opened the innings. Shyam had earlier taken seven of the fifteen wickets. And now the entire burden of getting to 178 was on him. While his team mates goaded him on, for the others it didn't really matter. They knew all the twenty overs would be bowled and even if all ten of them were dismissed there were plenty of monks waiting to swing the bat.

It was laugh riot part two. As Paras, a young, strong man came gracefully running to bowl, it was a breath-taking sight. He appeared to be a pro. But as soon as the ball left his shoulders, it was an anticlimax. It bounced five times and slowly came near Shyam who effortlessly dispatched it to the neighbour's fence. Everyone laughed, but not Shyam. He was absorption incarnate.

Venky ran up from the non-strikers end and joked with him a few times, but Shyam ignored it; he was focused. Soon Venky lost his wicket trying to lift the ball Kishor had bowled and was yorked.

Kishor came running down the pitch and apologized. "I am sorry, actually I had bowled a no-ball. You should continue batting." "No, I am out," Venky resigned to his fate.

Meanwhile Aki, the self-appointed umpire said it wasn't a no-ball. But Kishor insisted he had chucked the ball and that was a foul. So Venky played again but in the next over he was again dismissed, this time caught in the slips as he tried cutting a good line and length delivery. Other batsmen came, some entertained, others tried to be serious but slowly wickets fell. Shyam kept scoring runs on the other end and he soon reached fifty.

Another monk was absorbed in giving a loud running commentary of the match, which bought expert comments and laughter from everyone.

Gopal was chastising everyone and threatening that he'd win the match single handedly for his team. Suddenly as Kishor came running down the pitch, Gopal stunned everyone.

"What was that?"

He positioned his body square-on with the ball, both feet pointing towards the bowler at a perpendicular angle. It was even more surprising to see Kishor, a professional cricketer bowl a slow, short delivery which he effortlessly deflected towards the fine leg region.

"That's called Paddle-scoop, an unorthodox shot, condemned by the cricket pundits," Kishor loudly proclaimed.

Laughter again.

"Let me further educate all of you that Gopal just proved he's a genius cricketer, not everyone can play this shot with success." A thunderous applause followed amidst laughter, and Gopal raised his bat to acknowledge the cheers.

Kishor then took over the commentary. He ran all over the field and goaded his bowlers to get wickets. Venky turned to a friend in the stands, "Kishor's on a high, seems intoxicated by this game. I guess he could play cricket forever."

His friend remarked, "Poor guy should have played cricket for India but is struggling here in the ashram. This match is a poor consolation for him."

Meanwhile in a moment of misjudgement, Shyam hooked the ball a little too early and it was high in the air behind square leg, and Kishor came right under it.

Dropped!

"Kishor dropped such a simple catch," the commentator was back in action, "I think he too is influenced by the stalwart cricketers of our monastery."

The next over, Kishor bowled three full tosses at Shyam who effortlessly smashed them over the boundary. Kishor conceded twenty- five runs in the over.

The commentator was boisterous, "Shyam is threatening to take the match away from the jaws of defeat. He is on fire. He has now brought down the run rate to just seven an over. And Kishor is fumbling under pressure. Look how anxious he is, and is making last minute adjustments in the field."

"He's doing it deliberately," Venky turned to his friend, "But look at his face. He makes us feel as if he's serious. But No! I suspect, he wants it to be close so he's throwing loose deliveries."

"What's this, the most shocking decision by the captain," screamed the commentator as he jumped down the ground and sought attention to himself. It seemed important that the audience realize that his expert comments were precious. "It's Paras who's going to bowl the penultimate over. Kishor is risking losing the match."

Paras bowled outside the off stump. This time Shyam, instead of the regular sweeping of the ball towards the leg side, swapped his hands on the bat handle, and played a cross batted reverse sweep, and the ball went on the off side, to the third man boundary.

The crowd erupted with joy at this unorthodox batting display and roared, "More…we want more…"

Shyam hit every ball he faced with confidence and elegance. When he reached his century, Kishor ran and spontaneously lifted him. He urged the others to join, and they carried him on the ground. During the critical moments of the last overs Kishor's clumsy fielding surprised Venky. Others didn't care though, and Shyam's excellent batting took them to victory with a ball to spare. He remained unbeaten at 130.

As everyone laughed and frolicked on the grounds, Balram team members mildly chided their captain. "Kishor's overconfidence, his silly fielding mistakes and wrong decisions cost us the match," said one monk animatedly. "And what kind of a lousy captain is he, he was happy when the opponent scored a century and won the match for them. He's a traitor," others chided, and pulled each other's legs, recalled the funny moments of the match and there was a grand celebration accompanied by mocktails and special snacks.

The high -spirited match had ended, and Aki announced the honours.

He named Kishor as the man of the match much to the surprise of everyone else. Venky however knew it. Aki had recognized Kishor's acting. He appeared to be playing seriously but ensured the match was close and helped everyone else have an enjoyable time without them realizing it.

"It's a pleasant surprise to see you here." Shyam said to Kishor during dinner. The match was now over, and the dumbcharades game following the snacks ensured the monks forgot the cricket event. "I believed you were fasting, haven't seen you eat for days."

"This is an amazing feast," said Kishor.

Venky took Kishor aside, and said, "I feel proud of you Kishor, not because you played so well. But you let the others enjoy the game so much. And you didn't even let them feel that you orchestrated the run chase in such a way that they felt they had won the match with merit against a team that was led by a professional cricket champion."

"No...No." Kishor hurriedly dismissed it. "Shyam was brilliant. He has played professional cricket too. He was at top club levels. He would have surely played for Mumbai if not India if he wasn't a monk. I wouldn't want to take away the credit from him."

"That's true, he played well. But you played better. You were a cricketer when you batted, and then an actor when you fielded and a genuine, loving gentleman when you helped others win. I am so blessed I have you as my friend."

Kishor remained silent. Shyam joined in and said, "Aki isn't a fool to award you. He knew what you did. It requires great strength of character and a rich heart to let others have fun at the cost of burying your ego. You are a rare gem Kishor."

"I love you," said Shyam, and Venky too said aloud, "I love you also."

Kishor broke down. With his fingers, he swept off the tears and excused himself.

"Please, always keep me in your prayers," said Kishor as he retired to his room. "I need your friendship. I'd be the biggest fool to trade the wealth of this joyful association for the shallow pleasures this world can offer."

❑ ❑ ❑

PART - 3

CHAPTER 6

Kishor's Leaving the Monastery?

As the monks retired slowly to their rooms, Venky and Shyam caught the sight of Aki who relaxed alone gazing at the stars and silently fingering his chanting beads.

"Yes, I remember him, he hasn't changed at all in these eighteen years." Aki smiled recalling Kishor's initial days in the ashram.

"Is he leaving the ashram?" Venky asked.

Aki pretended to ignore the question and said, "He played so well isn't it. He reminded me of the stylish Tiger Pataudi. There is grace and royalty in his play. I think our ashram is too small a playground for him. He needs to do big things in life, not simply chant, pray and impart discourses. He is a leader, and we monks are simply servants with no material possessions. He is the son of a billionaire while we are paupers."

"But what's wrong with him? Is he in love with some woman? Why is he leaving?"

Aki's silence was interrupted only by the distant laughter of monks and the songs of the night birds.

"This is such a rare sound, isn't it," said Aki, "We don't get to hear the nightingales and the owls back in our south Mumbai ashram, do we?"

Venky twisted his face, and looked away. He was obviously irritated by Aki's old habit of beating around the bush. Shyam didn't seem to mind and feigned interest in the birds.

Shyam said, "I thought like the humans, birds also spend their night sleeping. I wonder why they chirp and hoot so loud."

Aki said, "That's obvious! We crazy monks are creating a hullabaloo in this quiet farm. And these poor birds are seeing us as prospective invaders. Fear, my dear friends, its fear!"

Some more moments passed. While Aki softly chanted on his beads, Shyam seemed to enjoy the pleasant breeze. Venky sighted Aki's mobile on the grass- an old Nokia model, a contrast to Kishor's high tech gadget. It was on silent mode as it rang. In the dark the phone glowed, and flashed 'Kiran'.

"Who's this Kiran, calling for Aki?" Venky thought for a moment, "Maybe he too has a girlfriend. I guess that's why he's not doing anything about Kishor. Oh, these are the closely guarded secrets of the renounced order?"

Aki who hadn't noticed his mobile ring, inhaled deeply, "Wow! Fresh air."

"Let's walk to the river bank," said Aki.

"Kishor had always been sweet and unassuming when he stepped into the ashram two decades ago. I remember he was big news. The monks were curious to know why a billionaire's son had come to dwell in the humble ashram. Somehow, he was attracted to my classes and would meet me often and tell me all about his family, ambitions and girlfriends. I became instantly fond of him. He was inquisitive about the philosophy too.

"One day I saw in the morning papers, Kishor's photograph with the caption, 'Kishor's scintillating knock takes ICM to the finals'. The article spoke about this talented eighteen- year- old whose blitzkrieg knock single handedly saved his team from defeat and powered them to a thumping victory. I was impressed and expected he'd share his exploits with me. However, he never spoke about his cricket achievements. And that surprised me. Most people would brag about their meagre cricket accolades and here was a young man in his late teens, with tangible credits to his name, yet he kept mum. I decided to investigate. The next time he came to the ashram, I asked him how his cricket career was unfolding. He didn't say much. I probed him further and what I heard then left me shocked."

The phone vibrated again. Venky again saw 'Kiran' but Aki in an instant picked up his mobile and excused himself.

After a few minutes of watching Aki at a distance, speaking on his phone, Shyam turned to Venky, "Oh boy, he's quite intense in his conversation. And it's 10.00 p.m. now. I wonder who the lucky guy is."

"A lucky girl!" said Venky.

"What, a woman again!", asked the bemused Shyam.

"Yes, I saw the call is from Kiran. Maybe what Smita is for Kishor, Kiran is for our Aki!"

Aki returned. Venky sensed his distraction.

"You were talking about Kishor's cricket career." Reminded Shyam.

"Hmm... yes. Kishor hated his parents' opulence. His dad had a flourishing textile and diamond business. His mother was busy partying. Kishor on the other hand loved to hang around with the simple and poor people. He had rich friends yet he wasn't happy with them. Once when I probed him on his passion for cricket he confessed to not liking cricket as much but played because he didn't know what else to do with his life. He told me about one of his friends who lived in the slums of Mumbai. The boy's parents struggled to make their ends meet; his father was a porter in the railway station and the mother was busy taking care of her young children in a dilapidated hut.

"Kishor often told me that his friend was a gifted batsman. However, he couldn't make it to the big cricket league because he didn't have the right contacts and often struggled to get opportunities to play regularly. Playing cricket is a full -time commitment which he couldn't commit to since he also had to earn a living, make some money to supplement his father's earnings. Kishor would describe the boy's ordeals in great detail. I was impressed to see him empathise so deeply.

"One day, Kishor told me that he was a mediocre cricket player compared to his friend. His friend wasn't selected for the under 19 team whereas Kishor had been selected as the captain and had been showered with a lot of praise and respect by his fellow teammates and officials. Later he found out that his father had bribed the team selection board to get him selected in place of his friend. He felt hurt but was helpless. When he confronted his parents, they dismissed the incident and tried to assure him that he was indeed a super talented boy who would surely play for India soon. But he told them that his friend was a better player and this annoyed them. It didn't take long for Kishor to realize his parents drew social mileage out of his cricket talent. They could tell their friends their son was a champion cricketer. His father pushed him to practice for hours and hired the best coach to train him in the back yard of his own bungalow in South Mumbai. Kishor claimed that he received a lot of opportunities to learn and play cricket.

"Once he cried while narrating to me that his friend had given up cricket because he couldn't afford to play. The boy's brother was involved in the underworld mafia and the police were harassing his family members. Besides, his father had turned alcoholic and there would be violent squabbles at home every night. The unhappy domestic scene sucked out the cricket spirit from his friend's heart. He did a few menial jobs to earn enough to maintain his family. Kishor felt pain for the less fortunate people of this world and we'd spend hours philosophising, why bad things happened to good people. He'd feel pacified in our ashram and the moment he stepped out of our premises, he confessed he would feel scared and hounded by the bad selfish world.

"One day I told him the story of Padmakar Shivalkar, an unassuming orthodox bowler who was one of the best in the country but could never play for India. Kishor had tears in his eyes and he'd relate very much to people who were good but not famous, those men who were effective but not glamorous were his real heroes. He was so excited and inspired when I told him about the legend of Sir Jack Hobbs."

"Who's that?" Shyam asked.

"Hey, you were a talented cricketer and you don't know Jack Hobbs?" Aki taunted.

Shyam shook his head sideways; he had no idea.

Aki continued, "Jack Hobbs is undisputedly the greatest cricket player ever. He scored over 61,000 runs and 199 first class centuries. Kishor was fascinated by him because Jack Hobbs was born in poverty and played cricket in a no -nonsense manner as a means of livelihood, always remaining humble and defiant in his batting because he didn't want to get out. And for him scoring runs meant living off his poverty. He always remained modest and humble in his demeanour and so shy was he of his own financial and social standing compared to his wealthy colleagues that he didn't even invite them for his wedding, thinking how could he expect the royal, big people to grace his modest marriage.

"Kishor would smile hearing this story and wryly contrast it with his own life. He said he felt choked in his own rich and fashionable life which was superficial and hollow. He felt so comfortable being with our humble monks in the ashram and to know that they possessed nothing, excited him. He'd often tell me that he too wanted to live meagrely and wondered if he could join the monastery. We laughed it off and I discouraged him, knowing he'd find it challenging to live without the opulent comforts of his house that he was used to. Ashram life is tough, so I thought. But he disproved me. He's been here for almost eighteen years, silently and effectively serving every day. Until of course now, when he's in a crisis."

Aki paused and seemed reluctant to continue. "Actually, since you are his good friends, I think I should share with you guys. Please don't tell him unless he himself reveals it. I don't want to break his heart."

"He had a girlfriend when he was a star cricketer. He once brought her to the ashram. She was beautiful, and looked like a graceful heroine, straight out of an old black and white Bollywood movie. I knew he was in love with her and would never leave her. He introduced me to her saying they were neighbours and family friends. That was the only time I saw her. Days later I heard he had proposed to her and she wasn't sure, there was some uncertainty.

I wondered would they marry or no? And suddenly one day I see Kishor standing in the ashram with his bags, saying he wants to be a monk."

"He has a streak of melancholy in him," Aki said thoughtfully. "I guess his liking for the deprived and lost souls got to him as well. This is the law of attraction. He lost his love and he joined the ashram."

"That's escapism, isn't it?" Said Venky.

"I don't want to comment on that," said Aki. But of late she's come back into his life, eighteen years later his love has revived. And now he's wondering whether to go back to her or stay in the ashram. His problem is he can't see others unhappy. He wouldn't mind if he's unhappy or even loses out on his desires but he can't break her heart. She wants to marry him."

"Oh no, he should just stay here. She's nothing but *Maya* -illusion, and a deadly power of distraction for monks." Venky was loud and emotional.

"*Arre nahi yaar*, I think he should marry her." Shyam sighed and said, "Lucky guy, at least there's someone who loves him and if he's happy let him go back to her."

Aki stared at the grass next to the river bank while the full moon danced on the gently flowing water. The light musical sound of the river's flow resonated with the occasional shrill whistles of the unknown insects and birds in the dark.

Aki got up and began walking back to the room. The duo followed quietly. No one spoke.

"Good night!" Aki said and retreated to his room.

By now the farm was silent. The monks-except Venky and Shyam- had retired. The two friends sat outside the room. They knew they wouldn't get sleep soon. "I fear it's not simply Kishor who's struggling. He has company," said Shyam.

Venky said, "I wonder who's this Kiran?"

The next morning, the penultimate day of the picnic promised more fun. But Venky and Shyam were still in bed. They seemed tired and emotionally drained at the prospect of losing their dear friend who'd soon leave the ashram. He was after all their good friend and confidant and had been their companion for over a decade.

"You both are still in bed? C'mon get up, you have an important job to do this morning." Gopal shook both of them from their stupor.

"Today evening we are returning back to Mumbai," Gopal announced, "And I want you to compere the last session to bid farewell to Kishor."

"No, I can't do it," Venky instinctively protested and looked surprised, "But the retreat was supposed to last until tomorrow, right?"

"Yes," Gopal said, "But Sinu's condition has worsened and doctors fear he may not survive another day. Since his house in on the way to our ashram, we thought we could all go there, sing kirtans for him and his family's spiritual well-being and encourage him on his final journey."

"That will be a double setback for many," Shyam said emotionless. "First we shorten the picnic by a day and then on top of it we announce Kishor's departure. I think let's not get hasty. Please wait for a few days till we announce Kishor's decision."

"Yes, give us one chance," Venky said, "We will convince him to give up that woman and continue here in the ashram."

"No, you won't do that," Gopal said, his voice raised in concern. "You can't force anyone to either join or leave the ashram. He is independent and we should encourage him to settle down in life if that's what he desires. Besides, he's desperate to move out."

"But please not today. Let us first talk to him. We are his friends. Let's get back to Mumbai and then announce. I am sure if he's stayed here for so many years he can tolerate our company for a few more days."

"I have already told him to talk to both of you," said Gopal. "He may meet you today before lunch. After lunch, we have planned his farewell address and then we depart."

"No, I suggest a small change," Venky said hurriedly. "Let's talk to him now and then before lunch, we can just give him a speech of appreciation and invite him to share his realizations of ashram life. But please no announcements and spoiling the ambience of the retreat. After he speaks, let's all rush to Sinu's place and then maybe next week, let's announce in the ashram. But I beg you not today."

"Well, if you insist," Gopal gave in to Venky's persistence. "But you both take care of him and we are shortening the retreat by half a day. We leave immediately after lunch."

❑ ❑ ❑

PART - 3

CHAPTER 7

Smita and Kishor's Love Story

Gopal and Aki announced about the rapidly deteriorating condition of Srinivas and the monks unanimously agreed to serve the family in his last days, and perform *Kirtans,* to help ease their pain and give them strength.

Then the regular morning class commenced.

Kishor, Venky and Shyam skipped the class.

Kishor told his friends, "I am sorry, I didn't tell both of you for so long. I am planning to leave the ashram and get married."

Venky and Shyam remained silent. They knew Kishor had more to share. Venky leaned forward, placed his palm on Kishor's hand and said, "We'll miss you but I am sure, you will be happy wherever you go. A gentleman that you are, your wife would be the most lucky woman to have you as a husband."

Kishor broke down and cried for almost five minutes while Venky and Shyam remained silent.

"I don't know what I am doing. I love you guys, but I don't know how fast this has happened. I shall be marrying next week."

Venky said, "That's good news Kishor. I wonder who that lucky girl is. Would you like to tell us about her?"

Kishor then narrated his story.

Smita was an amazing contradiction; bashful, yet assertive, modern and outgoing in her views and appearance, yet grounded firmly in family traditions. She'd appear vulnerable, one who needed my protection, yet took charge of the situation when it mattered. She'd communicate with her eyes, her affection for me. She was reassuring and expressive in love, yet reticent when I tried to get intimate.

She moved to our neighbourhood when I was eleven years old. She's a year younger to me. Her parents hailed from the culturally rich Shri Vaishnava community from South India. And being the Iyengar Brahmins, the highest in the social order, they were also pious and God fearing. Pre-marital dating was unheard of in their family although friendship and acquaintances with other boys was not uncommon. They spent their holidays and free time visiting sacred places, going on pilgrimages, visiting temples, performing religious rituals, or discussing literature and watching classical dance and music performances. My folks on the other hand spent their holidays on a cruise, or high up on the Swiss Alps or played Bridge and partied with the rich and famous and visited the race course.

Although not as wealthy as my parents, Smita's father rose to be a senior director of the Reserve Bank of India. Even her mother was highly educated and the parents drowned their little girl with unconditional love.

We met first in school and then grew up together with the other kids in the society. We also often walked back home together from school. We fought as kids but I noticed for the first time when I was thirteen that amongst all the boys, she always showed a special liking for me. Every few days she would get chocolates or sweets that her mother cooked or some toys and happily shared her stories with me. On Raksha Bandhan, popular Indian festivals where brothers and sisters share their love and duty for each other, she would tie a Rakhi-a sacred thread-around my wrist. Everyone in our society did that; it was more of a cultural festival where boys and girls would celebrate a brother-sister type of relationship even though most of them were not biologically related to each other. We would both look forward to the festival not because we shared the affection of a brother-sister but the idea of her offering love and prayers for my well-being and my lifelong vow to protect her fascinated us. I would give her gifts that day. Although she tied the Rakhi to the other boys in the school or the neighbourhood, I was always invited to her house for the occasion. She made me feel special. She rooted for me during my school cricket selection and hugged me for the first time when I was appointed the captain of the team.

We professed to be friends, and she never hinted at anything more. But as I turned fifteen I realized-maybe due to hormonal changes- that my heart would beat for her, and I was in love. I wasn't sure how she would react. I got fearful that she may not appreciate adding the conjugal element to our friendship. It was pure and innocent, and maybe she would prefer, it remains that way. Then when she didn't invite me home for the annual Raksha Bandhan festival, I took it as a hint that she too loved me. And when we won the inter-school cricket tournament she sat through the whole match and cheered me on when I scored a century and then gave me a long hug. That's when I kissed her on the cheeks, and she was shocked, yet happy. She hit me with her fists, hard on my chest, and shyly ran away. I was convinced that she loved me too.

The next week I proposed to her. She wasn't surprised, in fact she said she knew it was coming. I asked her if she would marry me. I was sixteen and she fifteen. Our parents were planning our careers and here we were, adolescents, discussing marriage. My father wanted me to become a world class cricket player and her mother was determined to make her a doctor. We were still in school and for the next ten years there would be no marriage. She didn't say anything for a long time and then finally expressed discomfort at the way our relationship was evolving. She cried and said she loved me but wasn't sure if there was any romance in it. I was confused. I tried to kiss her, but she gently pushed me and then she fell on my arms and held the embrace for a long time. She wet my shirt with her tears and said she'd never want to lose me. She suggested we don't turn our friendship into a love affair.

Our parents thought of us as good friends. She moved to a medical school. We wrote letters to each other and occasionally telephoned.

Those were the pre- mobile phone and internet days. There was a lot of excitement when she came home during her vacations. We would go for long walks on the seashore. She was candid and laughed unabashedly when she was with me. But in the presence of other men she was discreet.

My family had wealthy acquaintances and our social gatherings would be an ostentatious affair; liquor flowed freely, dances and ribald jokes were common. She on the other hand was used to a sober celebration. She knew although girls flirted with me as I was wealthy and a flamboyant cricketer, I loved only her and nothing or no one came close to that. She would often joke with me if I had found a girlfriend amongst the scores of girls that I was acquainted with. I would laugh it away but she persisted until I assured her that she would be the first one to know if I fell in love. And when I asked her if young men tried to get close to her in medical school, she would just smile mischievously, and shake her head. She knew she was beautiful besides being a talented singer and a confident debater. Most men were in awe of her, and only few dared to get close to her. She knew how to protect herself. Although I was a hero in my college and friends' circle, I felt puny in front of her. Yet she cared for my ego; she would humbly enquire about certain things from me, and then accept my verdict on issues without protest.

Her parents always honoured me and she would tell me later that they had high regards for me. Although liquor and drugs was common amongst my college friends, I never touched it because I knew Smita wouldn't approve of it. She would feel great happiness and pride in me to know that I lead a clean life while living amongst high society friends who lived a life of promiscuity. Once when I said I had smoked cigarettes with my friends and drunk a little wine she cried. I promised I'd never do it again. It was easy to please her. I just had to lend a patient ear to all her rants as we visited different temples and when I told her I had become a vegetarian just to please her, she felt flattered. Meanwhile she would pen poems, and express her affection through elegantly decorated gift cards. I would sometimes argue with her that it was not fair that she controlled me and my tastes. She would brush aside my pleas.

Her purity resonated an intense magnetism; I could never dare to physically push myself on her. There were occasions when we were alone for hours and yet we never got intimate. I did try but she would yield a little and then gently withdraw. She had great control on her emotions. She would apologize that she couldn't reciprocate my love. I respected her desires and left her alone. She would then give me a hug and say she was proud of me.

It was now six years since I had first proposed to her while passing out of school. Now I was a budding cricketer, who had just made it to the Ranji team and could soon possibly become a national hero. Meanwhile she had become a medical doctor and had blossomed into a beautiful young woman. As I carefully considered proposing to her again, this time seeking her hand in marriage, she informed me about a certain marriage alliance that had come her way. Her father had shown her the details of a particular young man, an accomplished heart surgeon from their own community, working in the US. Their horoscopes matched and the family was keen she meet him once. She told me she wasn't sure what to do. That evening we sat quietly on the Chowpatty beach for a long time. I knew it was now or never. If I wanted to marry her, I had to do it now.

I held her hand and said I loved her and asked if she would marry me. She looked confused and said she loved me but had never thought of becoming my wife. She felt I was her best friend, and assured me that it was an honour greater than being a husband. I never understood what that meant. I insisted we could be great friends even as married partners. She heard me patiently and then said that somehow her heart was unwilling to accept me as her husband. I screamed at her illogical stance; I cried while she sat patiently, yet impassively. She was kind to me. She said any girl who married me would be the luckiest woman, but she couldn't be my wife. I was wild. I admonished her, but I knew I couldn't force her. I loved her so much that if she didn't want to marry me, I would respect her wish. I quietly drove her home and she again apologized and I knew she was resolute in her determination.

That night I couldn't sleep. I was devastated. I cried and wondered what kind of a woman was she. Was she using me all these years? Was our mutual affection for each other meaningless? I felt so unworthy and humiliated. I knew this was the beginning of the end of my cricket career.

A few weeks later I chanced upon a flyer that advertised, 'Journey of Self Discovery course'. I was descending from the 'Hanging garden', a scenic park atop a small hill in South Mumbai when someone handed me this invitation. I would spend long hours alone in the park staring at the sky, wondering about life and death, trying to gather the broken pieces of my fragile heart. I would see young couples cuddled together in a secluded love nest. I'd remember the loss of Smita and weep alone. I was low on self-esteem and fared badly in the tournaments. Then this six -session course came along and I participated. I was stunned by what I heard. I realized there was more to life than my tragic love story.

Smita was gone but I had a pure soul and I could receive abundant love even without her. As my head spun at the magnificence of the Vedanta knowledge and my heart bathed in the nectar of the holy names of God, I felt nourished through my spiritual practices, I felt hopeful. I slowly managed to gather myself. My cricket game got better. I felt I could transcend my emotional trauma of having lost my childhood love.

Initially i avoided Smita, but slowly as i found shelter in my spiritual practice and my cricket flourished, I could perceive Smita as an innocent girl who had made her choice in life. She had every right to reject me and that didn't mean I was unworthy. I approved of myself and I thought I had transcended my attachment to her.

My meditation and study of scriptures gave me an insight into the temporary nature of this world. I slowly began to see through its superficiality. I thought I had attained some advanced stage of consciousness because romance, cricket and Bollywood didn't excite me anymore.

Then one night a strange reality hit me.

It rained heavily. I wondered why she had called me home. Her frantic voice on the phone convinced me something was terribly wrong. I saw my watch. It was 10.00 p.m. I was planning to join the monastery next morning, and had some last-minute packing to do and things to settle. I was at my uncle's house and wondered how she had got his phone number? She must have been really anxious to meet me once before I joined or maybe something else was the matter.

I had already been practicing strong spiritual principles for over two years now and my relationship with Smita was a formal one. We rarely met and exchanged only pleasantries. She was out of my mind and heart, so I thought. But her desperate call evoked compassion in my heart.

"Is everything all right?" My mind raced as I drove through the puddled streets of Mumbai. Somebody must have told her I am leaving home for good. But even my parents didn't know that. I had simply told my parents that I was going away for a six months training course. So there was no way for her to guess that I was on my way to becoming a *sannyasi.* Maybe her marriage was breaking apart.

"Welcome Kishor!" She greeted me pleasantly and handed me a towel to wipe off the rain water from my hair and face. Her smile was misleading. Having known her for so many years I knew her moods and heart better than anyone else. She was in pain but I could see she put up a brave face. Gone were her beatific and wide-eyed expressions that I was used to. Here she was; her haggard expressions and slow movements hinting to me that just six months of marriage had taken away her youthful beauty and added twenty- five years to her life.

I observed a sudden gush of emotions in my heart.

"Would you like some dinner?" she asked; she tried hard to look happy but failed miserably.

"I had my food and was about to retire for the night. What about you?"

"Some coffee?"

Before I could respond she murmured, eyes downcast, "Oh you guys now don't drink tea or coffee because of the spiritual inclination, right?"

"Where's your hubby? Your parents? And when did you come to

India?" I asked. I was in denial. My heart ached because what I really wanted to ask was, "Oh dear, what's bothering you?"

I wished I could once again hold her in my arms but now she belonged to someone else. I hoped she'd let herself loose on me and I could once again caress her free- flowing hair and reassure her, "Honey, I am always there for you; and don't worry everything will be all right."

She looked down, began sobbing slowly at first, and then with beseeching eyes, brimming with tears, looked up. Wiping off her tears, she spoke without emotion, "I am fine; my parents have gone to Tirupati, and my husband is returning the day after. I arrived last week."

"And what about you?" she spoke after a pause. "I heard that you don't play cricket anymore?" again she wept. She couldn't put up the pretence for long.

"What's wrong Smita?" I rose from the sofa.

"Oh my God, you are crying." I rushed, held her shoulders then instantly released her. I was reluctant. Could I do this? I am an apprentice monk who always keeps a respectful distance from women and money. But she was different. My heart always beat faster than normal when I thought of her. And the pent- up emotions over the last two years now began swelling in my heart.

We sat at a fair distance from each other and spoke nothing. The thunderous roar of my shattered heart deafened me to the rumbling clouds outside. The honking cars and screeching brakes were barely audible to us.

She needed care. Poor thing, she was starved of love. I knew from the holy books I studied that all love in this world leads to disappointment. But I hoped and prayed Smita had found true happiness. She was dear to the Lord, and I prayed that she would always feel protected and loved.

On her wedding night, I thought I had killed the Kishor who lived only for Smita. I put up a facade, smiled at the wedding couple while offering presents and posed for a formal photograph. A few hours later as I lay alone in my bedroom, the real Kishor rose from the dead. I cried madly; I was crushed at the reality that as I lay alone in my bed she would elsewhere make love to a stranger. He may be an accomplished surgeon and yes, their horoscopes matched but no one loved her like me. She was mine but I had lost her. I would do everything for her, yet she rejected me. The piercing shafts of her betrayal crushed to powder the boundless love that I carried for her in my heart. I banged my head on the wall, I beat myself with my bat, I screamed and yelled the entire night. The next morning, I woke up late and slowly began reorganizing my life. A week later, she was again out of my mind as the activities of the monastery engulfed my consciousness.

"You know Kishor, you have changed a lot," she was now accusing me.

"I am sorry," I said.

"I am not happy." She looked at me pleadingly.

"Oh, I am sorry," I leaned forward and held her hand.

She slowly put her crying face on my chest. I rubbed her back gently, kissed her forehead. She wept and I said nothing.

Moments later she rose. "Why are you joining the monastery? But why take *sannyasa* just because I didn't marry you?"

"No, it's just six months training. And you aren't responsible for this."

"You can't fool me Kishor. I know you better that anyone else. Although we were scheduled to come next week, I flew back immediately because a voice within me said you are leaving me forever. Ten thousand miles away on the west coast of America, my heart beats for you every moment. Please don't give up your family, friends and me."

I sat frozen. My head reeled in confusion. What's happening?

"My marriage is the greatest blunder of my life. On my wedding night, as Anand held me passionately, I felt unchaste. I am yours Kishor. He is a gentleman and he surely cares for me. But I should have married you. I have loved you all my life. I don't know what possessed me? How could I ditch you? I haven't forgiven myself."

I said, "You knew I could die for you, yet now I live without you.

Instantly she grabbed me, put her arms around me and held me tight. I could hear her quick breathing.

She wailed, "I am sorry, I am sorry I am sorry. Please let me live with you now. Don't leave me please I beg you."

"You know our culture abhors a married woman spending time alone with another man," I said, half-heartedly even as I kept her in my embrace.

As the rains outside abated, she looked up at me with expectant eyes. I had never been this close to her in many years. She moved forward, raised her face, and gently pushed her lips on mine.

What an irony! For years I had craved this intimacy, and with all my might and with extreme difficulty, purged out this longing from my heart. But now, here she was, offering herself to me. Why is destiny so cruel? This isn't right, I knew it. My heart and mind protested. But she was now all over me. Her gaze held me in a passionate trance, her fragrance engulfed my consciousness. I had never seen her pine for me in the fourteen years that I had known her.

I knew I had to act fast. This had to stop. In moments, our affection would blaze into an uncontrolled inferno, and cause utter destruction. I suddenly released myself from her torrid grip, stepped backwards. She paced forward, held me again as I let her go.

"Please stop Smita," I shook her vigorously and seated her on the couch.

"I need to leave, please forgive me. I love you but it's all over now."

She feebly protested and then gave up. As she sat alone crying, I rushed to the door, and looked back once. An intense urge rose in my heart to rush back to her but a power beyond me pulled me away. I left in frenzy; I was in a terrible turmoil and only weeks later the reality of the episode sunk in.

"She never called me again and eighteen years passed until recently another reality hit me, and this time fatally."

❑ ❑ ❑

PART - 3

CHAPTER 8

Kishor's Love Revives

I received a strange friend request on my FB. It was from an eleven- year old girl. Her face evoked love in my heart. She looked familiar. I saw her name, Kishori. That's me, I thought with an added 'I', a beautiful name for a girl that meant youthful. She addressed me as 'Uncle' and asked me to be her friend. I was captivated and instantly replied 'Yes'. She shared stories and photos of her friends and it was all lost in the flood of posts and messages that fill up my inbox.

On a few occasions, she wrote mysterious posts declaring that I had been her hero all her life. She then said she wanted to give me a surprise and meet me. I readily agreed and then one day my mother called me and asked me to come home urgently.

When I rang the bell, a young, beautiful girl opened the door. She was charming, dressed in a *Langa Davani* or a half saree, a traditional dress of South Indian girls. An elegant colour of half white and red skirt, a matching blouse and *dupatta* adorned her body. She also had fragrant *mallige*, jasmine garlands in her hair. A faint Shri Vaishnav marking on her forehead added divinity to her appearance. My heart melted. First time in my life, fatherly affection flowed from my heart. I couldn't believe I actually felt so much affection for a child.

"Kishori?" I exclaimed.

She beamed in joy, laughed and ran to hug me, 'Uncle, surprise!'

I picked her up and embraced her to my heart's content.

I then saw behind her, my mother. She stood next to a woman I recognized instantly.

I was seeing Smita after eighteen years. She had put on weight. She was dressed in a light blue sari and looked as stunning as she did eighteen years ago. Time hadn't yet ravaged her beauty.

"You are Kishori's mother?" I asked, astonished at the sudden revelation.

She stood smiling. I had met Kishori's mother thirty-two years ago, when as a ten -year-old she moved to our neighbourhood with the same liveliness and beauty that reflected now in her daughter. It was nostalgic.

"Incredible!" I exclaimed.

"Amazing, isn't it?" my mother said.

"Kishori dear, you are taking all of us on a ride in the time machine," Smita said.

Her voice hadn't changed in these eighteen years. She looked peaceful, and radiated a quiet grace. She had a purpose to live, and I guessed it was her daughter who now provided the fuel that kept her going.

"How, where, what and when? I have so many things to ask you but I am just overwhelmed," I said and sat on the floor.

My mother bought me water while Kishori opened her box that contained many photographs.

"You know uncle, you are my hero. Guess why?"

I was speechless. I had spent years listening to her mother's meaningless chatter but the deleted file had now been retrieved by this young girl. I said nothing, and simply looked at her with wonder while her mother sat at a distance, graceful and exuding unspoken affection.

"Do you know what your name means?" I asked little Kishori while looking at her mother, who shyly looked down.

"It means youthful but my mom says it means, a child dear to Kishor uncle."

"She named her daughter after you," said my mom.

Kishori had lots to say. "You know uncle; my mom says you were her best friend. I have heard so many stories about you, how you cared for her, protected her from so many dangers and loved her unconditionally. She always tells me I have to be like you when I grow up: pure and honourable." I felt flattered and loved.

Smita slowly walked to the dining table, "Lunch is ready, please come."

The last time I saw her she was distraught. Now she seemed to have come to terms with her life. Her facial contours reflected a painful history which I would know sooner or later. She spoke little while her daughter pulled me by the hand and shared all the chocolates and gifts she had bought for me.

"Your mom would give me the same kind of sweets when she was your age," I told Kishori while again stealing a glance at Smita. She smiled again and said nothing.

"I know uncle, she's told me all about your cricket, your parents, your friends and how you respected my mother more than any human being had ever done."

I thought my walking out of her house on that rainy night had hurt her but now I realized she honoured me for it.

"My mom says every boy should be like you and every girl should be like me." Kishori giggled.

Three hours passed. Occasionally I spoke to Smita but she said little; she seemed contended that she had seen me today after eighteen years.

But she did say, "I am grateful to you for who you are and what you mean to me is beyond my ability to express." My mom patted her on her back and turned to me, "Why don't you talk on the veranda for some time while I take Kishori inside?"

We spoke briefly and exchanged numbers and decided to meet soon. But I learnt that she had separated from her husband ten years ago, the first time ever something like that had happened in their traditional South Indian family. Anand's late- night work schedules and travels for medical conferences in the US landed him in a relationship with a Dutch woman from the East coast. Smita had caught him cheating on her and was even willing to forgive him for it. But he expressed his inability to keep his marriage going. They settled for a divorce and she had resigned herself to her fate. "I live for Kishori now," she quipped.

Her mother had died three years ago due to a brain stroke while her father at seventy, stayed alone in the same neighbourhood that they grew up in. She had decided to move to India with her daughter and stay with her father.

Over the next two months we met and spoke often. I carried gifts for Kishori and spent lots of time with Smita and her dad. He learnt some of our traditional meditation practices, and gained benefits from it. I taught the entire 'Journey of Self Discovery course' to Smita. She too chants the holy names of God and practices spirituality. She was already pious and now she took to my path naturally.

We even went on a pilgrimage to Vrindavan and Dwaraka for a few days with her family and my mom.

During this entire period, not once did Smita revisit our past. She was respectful and spoke to me as other women from our congregation would speak to a saffron clad, renunciate.

But slowly I began reminiscing about the past. She was reluctant, but I kind of pulled her into it. She would feel fearful and say, "You are a *sannyasi* now, and I guess in India, a monk doesn't entangle with women and money. So, I guess we shouldn't be talking about these things. I am sorry for disturbing you."

I repeatedly reassured her that she was an amazing lady and hasn't disturbed me in any way. But slowly the emptiness of my heart became obvious to me. I was practicing spiritual life all right but my emotional void was being filled by Smita and Kishori. I couldn't live a day without talking to Kishori. Smita told me a few times that maybe it's not healthy now for us to stay in touch.

But my need for a companion overwhelmed my heart. I realized all these years no one had loved me. I mean, I know Guruji loves me and so do both of you. I know Aki and Gopal love me too. But there is something only Smita can give me and that's not sex. There's something deeper, I don't know what it is but I feel incomplete without her and Kishori- whom I connect to as I would connect to my own flesh and blood. And I know I can't continue as a monk if I constantly seek her company.

I asked her to marry me. She repeatedly refused saying she didn't want to be the cause of a downfall of a monk. She even offered to shift to another city and leave me for good. I panicked at the prospect of losing her. I reassured her that it's my need, I wanted to marry her.

Kishor stared at the grass while the mid-day sun blazed above their heads. Then he finally said, "I know, I can never get friends like you but I need her. Please forgive me for letting you down."

❑ ❑ ❑

PART - 3

CHAPTER

9

The Farewell Address

Venky and Shyam sat quietly at a distance, the morning class got over and the last session of the retreat now began where different monks would share what had inspired them to join the monastery.

As Kishor picked up the microphone, Venky whispered to Shyam, "What an irony. Most people have no idea he's leaving us and now he's going to give a pep talk to the two hundred of us on the glorious life of monkhood."

"Please tell us how you abandoned cricket for God realization," one young monk raised his hand. Others cheered.

Kishor smiled and began his talk.

Venky felt nervous. He turned to Shyam. "He's leaving us next week, he's getting married to his childhood sweetheart and here we are being conned on the glories of monkhood. What an irony!"

Kishor began, "I was lonely and wondered about life and death; I'd also stare at the stars. Then one day I attended a class by Aki and the rest is history."

Loud cheer followed. Aki was a hero in the ashram, and many had similar stories to share on how they joined the monastery.

Venky pinched Shyam, "Now we have two tragedies. I am feeling a strange sensation in my stomach. First, the dramatic love story and now the glamour and glorification of Aki makes me uneasy."

Shyam said, "That's called butterflies. It's your flight response to the impending tragedy."

Venky said, "I am leaving, I can't hear this stuff. This sounds so hypocritical. Here he is planning to leave us and is glorifying another who is also entangled with a woman."

"Don't get up so abruptly," said Shyam. "Wait for a few minutes and then you could leave slowly."

Meanwhile Kishor continued, "After hearing Aki's discourse, I was fascinated by the teachings but not deeply convinced. I heard that we are insignificant and nobody truly loves us in this world except God. I secretly pooh-poohed this wisdom of the scriptures until one day when cricket showed me the dark side of this world."

"Oh, cricket again. Now I am not going" Venky said and looked serious like the others.

"My parents' cricket hero was Sunil Gavaskar," Kishor said, "My room was a dedication to his cricketing exploits. He was the highest run getter and had scored maximum centuries in test cricket and I had read all his articles and books. My dad would tell me that I would soon grow to be as great as him. One day as I came out of my jogging session from the park I saw Gavaskar right outside, looking anxiously in all directions. I rubbed my eyes in disbelief. I ran up to him and exclaimed that my folks were his greatest fans and dreamt their son would grow to be like him.

"I realized he was not interested in me or what I was saying. He offered a cursory smile and continued to look elsewhere while I blabbered on. That very instant I felt so unworthy and realized I meant nothing to him. Still being in the presence of a great man, I was inclined to serve. I asked him if he needed help. He said he was looking for a taxi. I ran helter-skelter trying to find one. In a minute, I was back with one and just then right in front me, I saw him board another cab and speed off. I wanted to talk to him, but realized he was gone. I sat on a bench nearby overwhelmed by this moment's association. My mind raced through a million things I could have told him but it was all over now.

"As I strained my eyes to keep trail of the taxi, the deluge of Mumbai's traffic soon consumed it. It was then that the painful reality of life dawned on me; he couldn't care less for my euphoria. I was indeed 'insignificant' and the reciprocation I desired so badly from him wasn't coming.

"That day the advertisements and bill boards looked so shallow. They declare we are the centre of the universe. Reality however throws up unpleasant surprises, and these occur quite too often to be dismissed as a pessimist's excuses. Meanwhile we march on, hoping that the next encounter with the 'real' world will turn things our way, and give us the much needed 'special' feeling, and the 'reel' world is there to keep us optimistic and positive. As we feed our consciousness with these self-centred and deceiving media images, we search for those moments and look for relationships that will massage our ego. Unfortunately, no one cares for our ego as much as they do for their own.

"Then at our monastery I heard the wisdom of the Bhagavad Gita; God is the most special person and each one of us is special as we are connected to him. But if we are disconnected from this abundant source of love, then not only do we feel 'insignificant' but all the heroes of this material world would also feel the same for they too would be washed away by the waves of time. But if we fix ourselves in our constitutional position of loving service to God, we'd transcend the petty hankerings and lamentations of this world. I learnt we are like a finger which is insignificant when separated from the body. However, when connected to the hand, it has a special place. A screw when separated from the machine is useless but when reconnected enjoys a unique function. Similarly, separated from the Lord, no hero worship can make our lives significant. We are like a fish out of water that cannot be lured by T.V, music or Coca Cola. The fish needs to be in water to really feel contended; likewise we won't be happy with the pleasures of this world, rather we desperately need to be fixed in our relationship with God to feel deep fulfilment.

"I also remember once as a teenager when Ravi Shastri was India's most famous cricket player, I saw him outside Mumbai's Wankhede cricket stadium surrounded by giggling teenage girls seeking his autograph. I was shocked to see the girls share ribaldry, and when one of them insisted on taking a souvenir from him, he said the only thing he had at that moment was the gum he chewed. She insisted she'd keep it as her treasure and then he spat it out. Immediately she caught it, and was hysterical. I couldn't believe those girls, and that somebody could be hero worshipped to such an extent. I felt disgusted.

"But in our monastery, I learnt that as opposed to modern heroes who may never care to know how much their fans love them, God, being present in the heart as the Super soul is cognizant of our smallest desire, and ever ready to reciprocate our longing and love for him. In fact, God is more eager to receive us in his loving embrace than we are, to feel the warmth of his presence in our lives.

"The day I joined the ashram, I wondered about these heroes I was leaving behind."

Then Kishor paused and Venky and Shyam shared a nervous glance. "I thought he was emotionally turbulent about Smita," said Venky, "I hope he doesn't speak about that now."

Kishor spoke softly, "I realized that if I am 'insignificant', so is a cricket champion, who a few years down the line will be bereft of all the media glare, and if fortunate, may avoid a disgraceful omission from the squad for a bout of poor performance. The plight of beauty queens, macho men, and political messiahs is no different. The most sensational heart throbs of the 80's, are unsung today, and replaced by a new bunch of attractive faces, only to be soon followed by another fresh set. Daily new heroes fill up the television screens, bill boards, and covers of leading magazines, and the country goes gaga over them. Meanwhile more young men and women are going crazy to follow these stars and etch their names in the flying pages of history. Precious human energy is thus wasted in vigorously pursuing ephemeral goals. Interestingly, our neighbour, China, the most populous nation in the world, has no clue about cricket, and its one billion plus citizens are busy with their own heroes. Seeing this maddened rat race, therefore, I often wonder, 'Is this endeavour really worth it?'"

Kishor stopped; his eyes brimming with tears.

Venky first clapped. Soon Shyam and others followed.

Gopal then called for other speakers.

Kishor came and sat in between Shyam and Venky. Both held his hand each, and offered a silent reassurance.

The program lasted another hour and half.

❑ ❑ ❑

PART - 3

CHAPTER 10

The Simple Joys of a Monastery

The lunch was a sober affair. Monks were speculating about Sinu's condition and wondered if they would reach his home before he breathed his last.

Venky sat alone in a corner. "I am not hungry," he said to Shyam and Kishor.

As the buses readied to leave the monastery, Venky came up to Gopal who seemed to relax in the first seat of the bus next to the driver.

"I need to talk to you and I am disturbed," said Venky.

"Oh, so you spoke with Kishor."

"Yes, but I am disturbed about Aki and Kiran."

"What?" Gopal instantly looked back and then sideways. He leaned forward, his eyes widened in disbelief, and Venky knew Gopal wouldn't want anyone else to hear what he had just heard.

"What do you know about Aki and Kiran?" Gopal's guarded looks and measured voice appeared probing.

"Is Aki entangled with her like Kishor is with Smita?" Venky asked.

Gopal smiled and then relaxed. He seemed relieved.

Venky said, "I am disturbed because Kishor is leaving. I thought monastic life meant no going back to the material world. Why is he leaving? And what's happening with Aki and Kiran. I saw them speak on the phone for hours. I fear the worst. If Aki too leaves like Kishor, it would be disastrous."

"Oh Venky, you are disturbed by Kishor's leaving. Don't' worry. Aki is fine. Kiran was his former girl-friend but don't worry and don't speculate. He isn't romancing her."

"I trust you," Venky said, "Both of you are equals and good friends; you have been in the ashram together for over thirty-two years; you have seen it all. I am inspired by your desire to serve in the monastery but I wonder why Kishor is leaving?"

"He's feeling lonely and needs a companion, a partner to love and feel loved," Gopal said.

Venky gently probed, "But is this a reality of monastic life?"

Gopal said, "Are you feeling concerned that you too might feel lonely as you get older in the ashram?"

Venky nodded his head in the affirmative.

"Yes dear, that's a sad reality but that doesn't mean everyone leaves and gets married."

Venky said, "But when I joined I was inspired to serve and pray for hours. I thought this would be enough to keep me going for the rest of my life. But seeing Kishor's change of heart and hearing you now, I feel nervous and unsure. I wouldn't want to leave the monastery when I am 45. If loneliness is a sad reality of monkhood, why wait to get lonely?"

The old Indian bus suddenly roared to life, and slowly rattled along the bumpy side roads. The horn blared as the bus picked up speed on the deserted, dusty pathways.

Both Gopal and Venky pulled up their hands to their ears, and squeezed their eyes shut. The monks grimaced, while Gopal who twisted his mouth and glared at the driver, shouted, "I can't hear myself think." The elderly driver returned the frown with his toothless smile and said nothing. Nonchalantly he turned the steering wheel to move the giant vehicle off the village dirt road towards the highway.

Gopal smiled, "It's a choice really. Either you get married or stay single; it all depends on what misery you chose. In my thirty- three years as a travelling monk, I haven't met any married man or woman who is completely happy. In fact, most of them envy our lives and think we are lucky to be not bogged down by the hassles of a nagging wife."

"But do you also feel lonely?" Venky asked. The moment he said it, he realized, he shouldn't have spoken that.

"Oh sorry," Venky's hurried expression said he meant it. "I know this is not the proper etiquette for a junior monk to talk to a senior. I am aware I was not even born when you joined the ashram. But I am of the modern generation which appreciates candidness and transparency."

"Don't worry. I am not offended."

Venky said nothing more, fearing he had already crossed the limit of propriety. Gopal stared out of the window as the bus vroomed, overtaking other vehicles. Venky saw the picturesque mountains and forests. He knew soon they would reach the outskirts of Mumbai, and the scene would change to crowded slums, rail tracks and people squatting on them, and the swarming buildings and imposing construction sites.

They passed a few minutes in silence. Venky felt the hot afternoon air blowing on his face from the open window of his seat as the bus sped at over 80 km/hr.

"Have you heard of the Spanish saint John of the Cross's, 'Dark night of the soul'?"

Venky had no idea.

"Hmm..." Gopal sighed, "We all have our moments of crisis and doubts; the journey towards God is not easy. A deep sense of meaninglessness can confront the best of the monks. Some pass through it in a few years while others like Saint Paul of the eighteenth century took forty- five years to recover from his dark night. Sometime ago I read an article in the Time magazine on

Mother Teresa, who's spiritual dryness lasted almost fifty years." Venky stared worriedly at Gopal who smiled reassuringly.

"Don't worry. These problems don't plague our married householders. Your grandparents I am sure never lost faith in God. Our ancestors lived in harmony with nature; they saw God in their work, family and community. We monks lead a rigorous and isolated life; I dare say unnatural for many. So, the obvious fall out is doubts and a prolonged period of dryness."

"Oh, so the householders are more God conscious!" exclaimed Venky.

"Yes", Gopal said and then winked, "but they have other problems. And for all the darkness that envelops a monk, paradoxically, you get closer to God. Your hankering for union with God intensifies as you tread alone on this adventurous spiritual path. So how can I trade this exciting voyage for anything else of this world?"

"I guess you are right," Venky said, "Our host, Mr Khanna spoke to me about similar things during the cricket match."

"Oh, what did he say?" Gopal laughed, "He's our old friend. Aki often teases him that he is a fallen monk."

"He narrated how years ago he stayed in our monastery for a week. Both you and Aki took good care of him. He was making some major business changes and had to stay a week in Mumbai due to some family and business complications. He didn't tell me the details but said he asked both of you what he should bring along from home. He was shocked when you said just get a pair of clothes, that's all. He then rose early with you guys, attended the full spiritual program in the morning, then participated in the ashram services and went out in the evenings for out-reach programs and then returned at night exhausted. He said he used no money during that period and had only one set of extra clothes. Today, twenty years later, he says those days were the best days of his life. He travels all over the world, has a loving wife and wonderful children, yet what he got in those seven days, he hasn't experienced ever since. He's bewildered when he recalls that he didn't even have money then, and yet what was it that filled his heart with purity and happiness that he's never felt like that all these years? He then looked at me and said we guys are really lucky to be living as monks."

Gopal smiled, "Yes, to live without money and women is not easy, but if you can, and then focus on God and service, then you have the greatest gift, you are the wealthiest human being. And you have the recipe for unceasing happiness. Mr Khanna is just one example, Sinu is another and he is the best of all. We will soon see him."

"But could I know who this Kiran is and why was Aki talking to her late at night?"

❑ ❑ ❑

PART - 3

CHAPTER
11

Aki's Past Returns

Gopal said, "Kiran and Aki were in a relationship while in college. He was a champion debater; his bifocals added a scholarly look to his six feet, semi-dark -complexioned personality. He spoke charmingly, and people loved to flock around him.

"Kiran was a few inches shorter than him. Her round eyes, fair complexion, and bubbly nature was unlike that of most girls from her Maharashtrian community. She usually dressed in traditional sarees or *salwar kameez* and her hair style was a classic bun or a simple plait. She often looked messy but was very attractive. Aki was a man of few words and graceful in his speech, she on the other hand was a striking contrast; a little clumsy in behaviour and boisterous in speech. Aki's silence attracted people to him while Kiran stole hearts with her spontaneous and loud expressions. She easily trusted people, and Aki was often protective, father-like to her. I guess as they say, opposites attract, and Aki and Kiran were in love. But destiny had other plans.

"She learnt about spiritual life first and then introduced Aki to Guruji. He got hooked, and like dry grass that catches fire instantly, he blossomed spiritually and realized he wanted to pursue it full time. He wasn't sure how to tell Kiran about this. He would come to our ashram and discuss with me for hours on what to do? I suggested he marry her because one's spiritual life wouldn't be inhibited anyway by marriage. But he was a man possessed. He finally told her about his desire to become a monk, and she broke down. But she knew his desire was pure, and he wanted to serve. She cried but wished him well. Since she was also spiritually strong, she could see the whole incident as divinely ordained. Aki's high moral strength and gentlemanliness had attracted her to him and now although she was torn by his decision to renounce the world for a spiritual cause, she showed tremendous courage and detachment. She proved her love for him, because all she wanted was, for Aki to be happy, even if she wasn't part of his happiness.

"As years passed, Aki grew in the monastery while Kiran remained a part of our community. They busied themselves in their services and had rare, formal exchanges. And she didn't marry.

Then one day, Sinu came up to Aki and said, the family welfare board of our congregation had proposed to him a marriage alliance. The girl was Kiran!

"Aki told me the next morning that he still loved Kiran and realized it only when her marriage with Sinu was on the cards. His heart ached, and this was ten years after he had joined the ashram.

He was thirty-one year old. He cried like a baby."

Venky's lower jaw dropped. "I can't imagine Aki crying."

Gopal said, "Love my dear friend melts the hardest heart. And Aki is a perfect gentleman; he wouldn't hurt an ant. Sinu was his best friend whom he had met in the ashram. He loved Sinu who offered menial services; he'd sometimes cook for Aki and then even stitch his clothes now and then. Maybe Sinu was like what a traditional Indian wife is. And here he was, marrying Aki's former love. Aki's emotional turmoil was natural, isn't it?"

Venky said, "Why should someone torture himself? He could have married her instead and they would have lived happily ever after?"

Gopal was philosophical, "Love again, my dear, is blind. When God attracts your heart, there is great excitement but pain is a part of the package. God's love is also irresistible. And by the way no married couple lives forever. Time inflicts fatal blows on every relationship, and a painful separation from your loved one is inevitable in this temporary world of suffering."

Gopal smiled, "The irony of it all is, it was Aki who actually helped Sinu marry Kiran. She wasn't sure of Sinu; her friends had discouraged her from marrying a former monk, who they presumed lacked social skills and they declared that life in a monastery makes one hard hearted, and Sinu would be a poor husband. Kiran was confused and she frankly told Sinu about her reservations. Sinu approached the wise Aki, and Aki's master stroke strategy helped Sinu win Kiran's heart."

"Wow that sounds exciting," Venky said.

"Aki asked him to find out about the women who had conspired against him. Sinu returned with the names of two older women from our congregation. Aki helped Sinu investigate more and soon he realized both the women had been irked by Sinu during his monastery days when he'd been strict in his dealings with women. They thought he was a male chauvinist who deserved no woman in his life. Sinu was disheartened. Aki encouraged him to arrange a lunch rendezvous with the three of them and scripted a perfect plot on wooing Kiran.

"Sinu learnt a few *shayaris* - Urdu love couplets for the occasion, to tease Kiran and present his romantic side to her. He also offered flowers to the older women, and was at his chivalrous best. As trained by Aki, he presented himself as a fool to the senior ladies, and happily asked them to punish him for his mistakes. He then went on his knees and petitioned Kiran to accept his proposal, while he showered praises on the duo for being so concerned about Kiran. He told them he was like their younger brother and humbly asked them to convince Kiran to marry him. He massaged their egos and let them feel important. They were pleasantly surprised to see this aspect of Sinu's personality. The ploy worked. Kiran was excited; she was in love again. Soon they married and lead a contended family life. Aki and I visited their house often and we were good friends with their children as well. Now twenty- five years later, he's dying of cancer."

"Oh, so the phone conversations are about Aki consoling Kiran?" Venky asked.

Gopal said, "Yes, and on the phone, he's also counselling and offering solace to the children. They love him dearly."

Venky said, "Aki must be really devastated; his best friend and Kiran and now death. How is he taking it?"

Gopal said nothing, he just sighed, then nodded his head. As a few minutes passed in silence, Gopal picked up his bead bag, and while moving the beads between his fingers, he silently chanted his prayers.

❑ ❑ ❑

PART - 3

CHAPTER 12

Feeling God's Love

"To tell you frankly, Aki is a saint. I am sure he loves Kiran even now. But it's spiritual love. They are connected as deep friends minus any conjugal feelings for each other."

"Is that really possible?" Venky asked curiously. "I have heard if a man and woman see each other privately, it's like butter and fire coming together. Could there ever be love without romance in a relationship?"

"Yes, it's difficult, but not impossible," Gopal said. "As long as you maintain a respectful distance from each other, it's possible to nurse pure emotions. But if there is proximity, then it's all a chemical reaction. You may keep the butter in the freezer for a thousand years, but once you take it out and place it next to a blazing fire, it will surely melt. Fire could keep your house cosy, yet it could burn it down. Similarly love keeps the heart warm with affection and purity, but if unchecked, it could destroy communities and shake people's faith. The worst in a man can be unleashed if lust isn't purified to shine as pure love.

"Therefore, for a monk to nourish love in his heart, he doesn't necessarily have to meet people all the time. In fact, he receives love not from this world but from God. His prayers increase his love deposits. Then he gives it to the people he meets; and that's a withdrawal. The men and women of this world, take spiritual love from a monk. Aki is smart enough to ensure he's always in surplus. His deep, heart-felt prayer sessions fill his heart with love and then when he meets the people of this world, he can impart love in abundance. His source of love is God, and the world is a recipient of God's love through him.

"And since you don't know the past, I must tell you Aki is my hero too. Many women came up to him and proposed to marry him. He is a brilliant scholar, orator and an attractive man. Yet he gently turned down all the proposals, wished the women well and cried alone seeking the companionship of God. He has chosen a life of solitude and prayer. And recently even as a fifty- five- year old man, Aki is so spiritually attractive and charismatic that a young lady offered to marry him. He politely declined the offer while keeping her honour and assuring her that she was a wonderful lady worthy of the best man in her life. He then chose to silently tolerate the pain of his own emotional incompleteness. But the joy of union with God, the feeling of warmth and love experienced occasionally during a prayer session, although in small quantities, makes us older monks feel special. That's when we feel that the whole endeavour is worth the pain."

"Besides the prayers, what keeps him going?" Venky asked, "Who or what inspires him to remain strong? And despite having no companion, how does he manage to give hope and happiness to everyone he meets?"

Gopal said, "Many of us are inspired by the monks living in Udupi. Have you been there?" Venky shook his head.

Gopal said, "It's the most incredible place for a monk to visit. Aki and I travel to Udupi once in six months, spend a couple of days in the spiritual oasis there. We recharge our emotional batteries and come back to this crazy city of Mumbai to continue our services.

"Udupi is a holy town in the state of Karnataka, the Southern part of India, where for over seven centuries celibate monks have dedicated themselves to the worship of Lord Krishna. The Krishna temple there was founded by Sri Madhvacharya who initiated eight disciples into *sannyasa*, renounced order, and they carried the legacy of Krishna worship. Each of these eight sannyasis has headed a disciplic line of succession and since the thirteenth century, each of these lines has yielded over thirty lifelong celibate sannyasis serving selflessly."

"Inside the temple complex at Udupi is a small memorial 'Vrindavan'. The bodies of seventy to eighty of these sannyasis' are placed there. It's one of the holiest places that many celibates visit for prayers and blessings. It is most inspiring to know that such pure souls served here for decades without desiring anything material. Most of these *sannyasis* renounced home and material comforts before they were even teenagers and then lived as a renunciate till the age of eighty to ninety. Standing inside the complex one feels a tremendous surge of inspiration seep in; a desire to serve selflessly.

"Most of the memorials built have no name on it. These *sannyasis* are silent servers who quietly serve the Lord, rejecting the ephemeral glamour and fleeting promises of the material world.

"One tomb particularly has caught Aki's attention and he never fails to offer his respects. It has a tiger's face engraved atop the tomb and belongs to Raghupravira Tirtha swamiji, the twenty third in the line of Palimar Mutt, (one of the original eight founded by Madhvacharya) who lived in the late 18th century. He lovingly served Lord Krishna in the temple and one day was disappointed to find a cow missing from the cow shed. This cow was swamiji's favourite and he offered the milk of this cow for bathing the deity of Lord Krishna.

"On searching, it was finally discovered that the cow had been devoured by a tiger in the forest. Disappointed that the cow's milk wouldn't be available now for his dear Lord, the swamiji repented and sat outside the temple fasting, as atonement for his disservice to the Lord. The news spread far and wide. As people gathered to see the intense penance of Raghupravira tirtha Swami, the towns' people were for a big shock. Right amidst them, as if from nowhere, a tiger appeared. As people ran in fear and later saw the spectacle hidden from the tiger's view, the tiger walked up straight to the swamiji in front of the temple. This was the same tiger that had eaten the cow a few days ago.

"The tiger too was affected by the penance and repentance of the swamiji and felt sorry for having eaten Lord Krishna's favourite cow. As an act of atonement, the tiger approached swamiji and while offering prostrated obeisance, laid down his life. Everyone was stunned to see a tiger give up his life in atonement. The swamiji then stopped meditating and fasting and resumed his services to the Lord.

"To commemorate this special event, the tomb of Raghuvara Tirtha swamiji has a tiger's face carved on it. Like this, there have been over two hundred and seventy swamis during the last seven hundred years who have served in the sacred town of Udupi. These souls have rendered selfless service and performed many miracles too. But their primary focus has been to remain in the background and humbly serve.

"And Udupi is just one amongst the many places in India where pure souls live and love God and then share that love with the human society.

"But my dear Venky I wonder what inspired you to join the monastery? Was it spiritual curiosity or an escape from suffering caused by a broken love life?" Gopal laughed as he probed the curious Venky.

Venky flustered and then looked outside the window. The bus was now inside the city, the horns blared loudly while the rustic driver hurled expletives at the other vehicles for slowing down the traffic. The bus jerked, then stopped abruptly, and again pushed forward. The monks felt at home.

Venky smiled sheepishly, "Well, I joined not because I really wanted to be a monk. I saw my childhood cricket dream fulfilled here."

Gopal's said nothing at first. Then he squinted his eyes and said, "There's no cricket here in the monastery. The retreat is over and we have never played cricket before."

"Well, no, I know that. I saw all of you live in the monastery and I'd see my favourite cricketers here," said Venky.

"I am all ears," said Gopal.

"Since childhood I have been fascinated by the Indian cricket team. Not so much for their sporting skills but for their ability to accommodate each other. I often wondered as a teenager how the eleven members of a team stayed and travelled together when their language and culture differed so much. India's diverse culture has been shaped by many religions, languages, castes and customs. Each of its twenty-eight states has a unique diet, architecture, dance, music and traditions. How can these eleven be united; what do they talk and share; how does a south Indian communicate with a Sardar from North India who knows only Hindi? These questions intrigued me and I would devour cricket magazines to know how this highly heterogeneous group had men sharing friendships and camaraderie with each other.

"The mystery got solved when fifteen years ago I began frequenting our ashram where I got a first-hand experience of living with different people. There I saw many monk apprentices serve, study scriptures, share the knowledge with others and devote their time to exclusively develop their love for God. I saw them practice celibacy joyfully.

"I soon realized, this is a more exciting group than the Indian cricket team. A cricket team has only 11 to 14 members belonging to the various states of the country, but they hardly stay together for long; inclusions and omissions from the team is a common occurrence. However, our ashram of monks is unique for we have over hundred distinctive individuals coming from not only the far and wide corners of India but also from foreign countries. This is an international team with each member having his own set of likes, dislikes and idiosyncrasies. Besides, once included in the team, they don't leave that often; they are here to stay. What keeps them united and how they struggle and adjust with each other, sharing joys and sorrows in a bond of loving friendship is a happy and instructive lesson to learn.

"When I joined in March 2006, as a twenty-three-year-old, I was amused to see the happy blending of dissimilarities. One particular contrast is fresh in my memory: Murugan, a twenty-five-year-old man is from a devotional, priestly family from Chennai, the Southern part of India. He was inclined to study the scriptures deeply and was ambitious to share the message with all. His partner in the temple cleaning services was Bhagat, a forty-five-year-old semiliterate business man who hailed from the Western corner of India, Rajasthan, bordering with Pakistan. He was more inclined towards physical services and was hard working. He didn't speak a word of English and Murugan couldn't converse in any other language with him. I would laugh at their clumsy goof ups and innocent misunderstanding. Being older in age, Bhagat often reprimanded Murugan for his mistakes. However, being unable to decipher the Hindi language, Murugan often thought he was being appreciated and would repeat the mistake much to the annoyance of Bhagat. Meanwhile most of us had a good time at their expense. Today, ten years later they are good friends and Murugan has picked up Hindi while Bhagat, now understands English. Both happily recall the old days and thank Lord Krishna for this wonderful arrangement. If not for a spiritual cause what would have ever brought us strangers together?"

Gopal smiled, "That's an amazing realization. I could add to it, if you permit."

"Please," Venky said.

"Everyone in a cricket team is important – the wicketkeeper, the fast bowler, the spinner, the middle order batsman and the openers. A match is won by each of their combined contributions. Similarly, in an ashram set-up there are front line preachers, great singers, *kirtaniyas*, good managers, efficient *pujaris*, and experienced cooks. Yet a happy and vibrant ashram is a contribution of all of their unique efforts."

Venky said, "I am glad you shared so many things about Aki. Trust me, it will remain confidential. But I also want to know what keeps you going? You too have spent over thirty years in the ashram. Who is your inspiration?"

Gopal said, "Aki introduced me to one special soul during my first Udupi visit some twenty -five years ago. I remember him even today and he gives me strength to pursue my spiritual life, alone, knowing there are great souls whose footsteps I need to humbly follow."

"I was one of his secret admirers until recently, when I spoke to him for the first time, and then my reverence multiplied many times over. What I observed and learnt from him left me impressed and inspired to serve with discipline and dedication.

"I am talking about VishwaPriya Tirtha swamiji, head of the Adamar mutt, one of the principal eight temples that manage the worship of Lord Krishna in Udupi. Each time I travelled to Udupi, I'd see him lead a simple life, chant alone in the temple during early hours with great intensity and devotion. I would also see him incessantly chant the holy names of Lord Narayana. Even while talking to others, he'd softly utter the holy names. That had become as natural to him as breathing is to us. At the same time, he was always present in his conversations; whoever meets him is touched by his endearing personality.

"Vishwa priya tirtha swamiji took sannyasa, the vow of celibacy and selfless service to God and humanity, in June 1972. Over the last forty -three years he has been serving the temple and his community tirelessly. His day begins around two thirty in the morning. He completes his chanting, prayers and worship of the Lord by nine in the morning. He then does yoga, keeps himself abreast with current affairs, teaches Vedic scriptures to a few students, and studies till lunch. After half an hour of rest, he meets guests, and rushes off to lecture in the evening. Then again, he meets guests and does his night *puja*, before retiring, usually after 10.00 pm. This has been his schedule for decades.

"He offers simple, practical tips to people who approach him with questions regarding family, business, or spiritual life. Each time I meet him, I touch his feet out of reverence and spontaneously he calls out, 'Narayana' and refuses to accept monetary donation, saying, we better offer it at the temple donation box.

"He speaks fluent English and Hindi which was also a revelation to me. His strictness with himself is well known but I was amazed to see he's accommodating and lenient with others. Last time we went with a group of five devotees, a couple of them were householders from our congregation. As we spoke, one of them expressed that he was unable to devote so much time to spiritual life because of his family responsibilities, to which swamiji replied, that at this point of time, his service to family was important. God would understand his predicament, he reassured. 'However, when your children are old enough and your responsibilities taken care of, you could increase your spiritual commitments', said Vishwa Priya Tirtha swamiji, 'and at that time if you are complacent, God will not accept your excuses'.

"During our two -hour conversation, I expressed my difficulty in controlling my tongue; I love to eat palatable foodstuffs, and I asked him if he could share some tips by which I could regulate my tongue. He blushed like a child, and then laughed innocently, 'We are vaishnavas, and we love to honour God, Krishna's Prasad. I too eat a lot, and am unable to say 'no' when there are so many delicacies'. He again laughed disarmingly and charmed my heart. For someone so senior and well acclaimed for his discipline and rigorous spiritual practises, it was the uncommon simplicity that touched my heart. Throughout the discussions, not once was he authoritative, although he was qualified by age and spiritual position. He spoke on principles, and as he rushed for his class, he requested us to pray for him.

"As we left the quiet Adamar mutt in Udupi, I was happy to have met a great soul. I also realized why he was spiritually so advanced and attractive to many seekers. His unpretentious, simple nature makes one think spiritual success is within our reach. Notwithstanding his intense practises, he made the path of renunciation appear simple and within reach for the simple hearted. I left humbled, and inspired, eager to follow his footsteps."

Gopal remained silent. The bus moved into the society where Sinu stayed with his family.

Venky turned to Gopal again, "I am grateful you shared these stories with me. I was a little taken aback by what Kishor did, but now I know monkhood is also a practical reality; it's possible.

"Renunciation is a glorious practice if one can do it."

Gopal nodded approvingly, and the monks prepared to get off the bus.

❑ ❑ ❑

PART - 3

CHAPTER 13

Sinu's Final Journey

The house was crowded with hundreds of members from the congregation, all assembled to chant and pray for Sinu as he now prepared to leave this mortal world. As the fifty plus monks alighted from the bus, the house came to life.

Sinu had expressed a desire to leave his body at his own home which was like a sacred temple. The deity altar was gorgeous and the spiritual atmosphere that he, along with his wife Kiran and his children created at home, gave hope and inspiration to many. The family taught by their own example how one could spiritualize one's household life. Since the last one month, Sinu had lain on his bed at home, surrounded by family and friends. By turn different members of the congregation sat next to his bed chanting prayers, and reading from the scriptures. Meanwhile many of his friends visited and shared spiritual thoughts with him.

Aki and Gopal along with others had come often to meet him. Doctors had expressed that today could be his last day, any time now and within the next twenty- four hours his soul would depart. Although the cancer had spread rapidly and his body was emaciated, he and Kiran had come to terms with the reality.

As Gopal and Aki briskly walked ahead, Venky kept pace. He didn't want to miss any of the action. Seeing the two senior leaders of the monastery, other devotees offered pranams, and rose from their seat.

Standing close to the bed, Aki with tear filled eyes gazed at Sinu. Venky was gauging the situation closely. Gloom filled the air, yet behind the sullen faces, there was spiritual peace. Gopal took the cymbals from a devotee chanting *kirtans*, and he began to lead the prayers. The chorus got louder; the devotees and now the monks too chanted with feeling. The entire room reverberated with transcendental vibrations.

Venky felt no emotion. He was curiously glancing at Aki, then at Gopal who with his eyes closed, chanted intensely. Then Venky's eyes fell on a lone woman in the room, who stood at a distance. He guessed she was Kiran. She looked much older than what he had imagined a few hours earlier in the bus when Gopal described her beauty. Holding back her tears, she gently caressed her teenage daughter who breathed heavily, crying at the imminent separation from her father. Kiran looked graceful, and Venky then saw Aki who looked misty-eyed at Sinu's teenage daughter holding her mother's arms.

Venky thought of how destiny plays funny games with the lives of people. Here was Aki standing so close to a lady who could very well have been his wife. But here she was, on the verge of becoming a widow, and Aki was crying at the impending death of his best friend. Venky's thoughts went back to his own college infatuations and how he had joined the ashram a few years ago, not having the faintest clue about the inner lives of his ashram heroes.

Although various pipes and masks covered Sinu's face, he looked radiant. He was breathing slowly, gasping for breath as he struggled to inhale. He opened his eyes, gazed at the room and then again closed his eyes. Venky knew any of these glances could be Sinu's last. Having never seen death in his life and only occasionally hearing of a distant relative's death, this was turning out to be a historical occasion for Venky. He tried half-heartedly to feel emotional, but was unmoved. His thoughts went back to Kishor who would be leaving the ashram to marry his childhood sweetheart while Aki was standing next to his former love who he had left to pursue a life of renunciation. The paradox confused Venky; his head reeled.

"Look, he's trying to say something," a devotee noticed Sinu was moving his body.

Venky saw Sinu had opened his eyes and gave a half smile. He moved his right hand and raised the left, an inch off the bed. He slowly turned his face to the left where Aki and Gopal stood chanting prayers. On his right was Kiran and their two children.

Immediately Kiran came close, gently touched her husband's shoulder and now Sinu turned towards his wife. Moments later, again he moved his head on the left and bought both his hands close to his chest, lifted them and joined the fingers of both hands in air.

"What is he trying to say?" Gopal interrupted his singing and exclaimed aloud.

Aki continued to cry silently, while Gopal resumed his *kirtan*. Venky stared at all of them.

Sinu's hand movements now became vigorous. Kiran continued to comfort her husband, and Venky watched in silence.

The devotees in the room stared at Sinu. Venky had heard many spiritual discourses on death but this was real. His heart beat fast and he nervously looked at the others.

Venky noticed Kiran's eyes meet Aki's. They acknowledged each other, and shared a melancholy bonding. Although they said nothing, Venky caught the poignant scene. He knew that instant they still loved each other. But then he reasoned it was a different kind of love. There is no romance here, Venky deciphered, but seeing Aki's wistful face, he wondered if Aki still longed for her. "Maybe he's thinking, 'if only things had gone differently'".

Venky then chided himself for his disgraceful thoughts. How could he imagine such bizarre things when death was so cruelly snatching away their beloved friend? Surely, they had transcended their college attraction. Life was now teaching them deeper lessons in friendship and sacrifice.

As Sinu twisted his hands in a snake like fashion, he was desperate to communicate something.

Kiran repeatedly raised her eyes pointing towards Aki. Aki looked quizzically at her while her children closed in on their mother. Sinu lay on the bed and continued his hand movements.

"He's writhing in pain, call the doctor. He wants something" said Gopal.

"No!" Kiran said, looking at Aki, "He's pointing towards your shirt."

Venky saw Aki's saffron *kurta*, a traditional monk shirt, clumsily adorning his torso. The three-day retreat had muddied it and the top button was missing. During an animated fielding session, Aki had collided with another monk, and in a desperate bid to grab the ball the young *brahmachari* had accidentally torn Aki's *kurta* near the collar and a button had come off. Aki nor the other monks gave a thought to it and the match resumed with passion.

"Oh," Aki said, "It's torn here, all right."

Kiran said, "He wants to stitch it for you." She squeezed her eyes shut as tears ran down her cheeks.

Gopal suddenly stopped his singing. Aki stood still and gave up the fight to hold back his tears. Another friend of Sinu gave out a loud wail. Venky was stunned to see his hero cry like a child. He realized his own eyes were also now brimming with tears while Aki looked skyward, sighed, and then again looked at Sinu.

"Yes, my dear Sinu, here take this shirt and stitch it for me by tomorrow." Aki's voice cracked with emotion. He said it aloud, giving vent to his pent-up emotions. He then made a half-hearted attempt to remove his shirt, and smiled ambivalently. He broke down again and held on to Gopal's shoulders, who lead the kirtan with feeling. But now Gopal too choked, and sang a discordant note while the cymbals played inappropriately to the melody he sang.

Aki smiled one moment, and the next, a deep sadness clouded his face.

Three hours later Sinu breathed his last, surrounded by his friends and family chanting devotional prayers.

❑ ❑ ❑

PART - 3

CHAPTER

14

A Monk's Secret Wealth

Venky's mind constantly reflected on Aki's words. "A monastery is like an ocean; a *brahmachari* is like a ship. While ships sail in and out, the ocean remains calm and steady."

He thought it was a profound statement, but it didn't really assuage his sad heart. It was three weeks since Kishor left the ashram. The farewell announcement was an emotional affair. Shyam cried while Aki and Gopal- the senior leaders of the ashram-spoke appreciatively of Kishor and thanked him for all the services he rendered for eighteen years. They wished him all the best and a few others spoke about Kishor.

New members of the ashram sat stunned, not knowing whether to feel sad or happy that he was changing his ashram- he was now moving from the monk ashram to the householder ashram. Venky felt emotionless then. He had wondered if he was a hard-hearted person but slowly he began to miss Kishor's presence and now the reality of his absence had sunk in. Kishor was one of his dear friends and his absence in the ashram was palpable.

This morning he rose early to clean the temple hall before the morning prayers. It was 4.30 am and slowly the monks readied for the *mangal aarati* that would start in half hour. Meanwhile as he swept the floor with a long- handled broom his thoughts raced back to Kishor. How one night, a few weeks ago he had seen him talk to Smita on a phone under an almond tree and soon discovered he was marrying her. Yesterday they registered their marriage in the local court and a few of their family and friends attended the small function.

Venky felt pangs of loneliness creep inside his heart as he now mopped the floor with a wet cloth.

"Are you all right today?" Aki asked. Aki was sweeping the floor of the adjacent hall and had seen Venky forlorn during the early hours.

"I am all right but missing Kishor and reflecting on what you said about the ashram being an ocean, and the monks, ships."

"Hmm but I guess philosophy makes no sense to an aggrieved heart," Aki said.

Venky continued mopping and he again looked at Aki who seemed to quietly enjoy his job of cleaning the hall. For over thirty-three years now, he rose daily at 3.00 am and cleaned the temple hall the first thing in the morning.

"If he wasn't a monk, maybe he'd have been a director of some company and would have servants clean his house," Venky thought to himself "And his beautiful wife Kiran would attend to all his needs. Together they'd make a lovely pair but now she is a widow and he's wasting his life doing menial service such as cleaning the temple hall which anyone else, even an illiterate man could do. What a waste of talent."

Venky felt uneasy at these thoughts. He knew the truth that menial service is the greatest wealth a monk possessed. And the happiness he himself experienced after cleaning the toilets or washing the thousand plus plates on a Sunday afternoon after the weekly festival, surpassed the pleasures of this world.

And Aki was a true billionaire! He loved rendering all kinds of menial services and at the same time, read scriptures proficiently and taught them to one and all. He served even those who were decades junior to him in the monastery. He felt no pride in being a senior member. This, Venky knew is the secret of a happy monk; he possesses nothing except the wealth of service. And that service nourishes him and dissolves the desire to control and exploit others. In his meagre experience of the ashram, Venky had on many occasions felt that control is the antithesis of love, and monkhood is a glorious saga of loving service.

Aki walked past him again and said, "Remember what you choose to think in the morning sets the ball rolling for the day.

Choose positive thoughts now and see your entire day go well."

Venky faked a smile and said, "Yes, thanks."

The Morning Prayer was led by Manik, a fifty-five-year-old veteran who sang and danced with the gusto of a twenty-year-old youth. Venky then thought of other monks who looked blissful and absorbed in their spiritual activities.

The secret of their joy, Venky often concluded was the spirit of giving. Whoever stayed happy in the ashram was because he always thought of giving. There was no place for one who sought to be a grabber.

Venky had also experienced that whenever he sincerely appreciated other monks, he felt rich, emotionally. Manik sang *kirtans*, managed the accounts, and served breakfast and dinner daily to the hundred plus monks. And remembering these qualities and seeing his enthusiasm, Venky now began to feel happy.

Aki slowly came from the side and placed his hand on Venky's shoulders and whispered, "Oh, you are smiling to yourself now. Good to see you are fighting it out."

"Yes, I chose to be positive," Venky said.

"Would you like to share your positive thoughts? I need it badly." Aki said.

"Yesterday in the morning, I had assisted Manik in serving the *Dwadashi* breakfast and felt amazed at his consistency and dedication to serve."

"Thanks for sharing this," Aki said and slipped away to his position to absorb himself in prayer. The monks closed their eyes, and folded their palms in supplication as they stood in rows and responded to the lead singer's kirtans.

The *brahmacharis* had fasted the day before for *Ekadashi*; every eleventh day of the waning and waxing moon, spiritualists abstain from consuming grains and absorb themselves in rendering various devotional services. The following morning, the twelfth day-called as *Dwadashi*-they honour breakfast with the zest of a young boy; the hunger of the belly invokes the appetite of youth within them. "At such times," Venky told himself, "It's inspiring to see monks like Manik who are content in serving others first before eating themselves to satisfy their own hunger."

Although the fare was simple- rice, vegetables and a few sour and sweet savouries to spice up the menu-you couldn't blame one for eating first rather than serve. And that's what Venky often did. Manik's mood however was rare, and that set Venky thinking on what actually brought happiness in the monastery.

Venky later met Shyam and recalled an incident when he learnt the lesson of giving, in a special way.

"After I joined the ashram my ever-concerned mother would get me a dozen mangoes every week. I would relish those mangoes alone in the ashram. Although solitude is rare in our monastery, I'd manage to find the time when no one came near my locker where I kept all my belongings. I'd then quietly take out one mango and enjoy it all by myself.

"One day as I was about to consume the mango, Parameshwar came around and saw me eating. I offered him one mango as an act of courtesy, albeit reluctantly. Soon Deepak turned up and I took out another one from the bag. In five minutes, we were a group of six to seven monks relishing the mangoes happily. Later as all dispersed to render their various services I felt a special gush of happiness flooding my heart. I had never felt the same all these days when I was eating the mangoes all alone. I immediately realized it was the act of going beyond the self, of sharing, that made me happier. I could clearly see the contrast in the experiences of quietly seeking to satisfy my own senses and now forsaking my own pleasures, although it was a simple mango.

"In life when we relinquish something for a larger good, we emit much positivity and that energy bathes our own consciousness with serenity and contentment. Manik reminds me of what our spiritual master always says, 'Wherever we find an opportunity to serve without expecting anything in return, that's where we are going to find the deepest experience of God.'"

"There's something higher than that." Shyam teased Venky.

"What could that possibly be?" Venky asked.

Shyam said, "What gives Aki a kick really is his happy willingness to forego any credit for his service. He feels joyful in being the anonymous benefactor."

"I don't think I can ever do it." Venky said.

"Me too." Shyam said.

"But that's why I guess we are the confused monks whereas he's the self-realized one." Venky declared conclusively.

Shyam smiled and said, "Once Gopal told me that for weeks he observed that the shoe rack was dirty and our brahmacharis just threw their shoes all around the shelf but not on the designated rack. He was tired of correcting the erring monks until one day this problem magically stopped.

"Every morning Gopal observed that the ledge was spick and span; the shoes well placed in the designated boxes and the surrounding area clean. By sunset however it would be a mess again. But the next morning it was again neat. He wondered who cleaned it up at night and even asked the ashram inmates. No one claimed responsibility. One night, Gopal decided to take up the matter himself. He stayed awake and hid himself behind the door. He was shocked to discover that at 1.30 am when the whole ashram was fast asleep, it was Aki who quietly did this service for half hour. Not wanting to disturb his sentiment of service, Gopal hasn't told Aki that he's aware of the culprit."

Venky laughed, "I doubt if the world outside would believe such human beings exist? I once probed how he could find joy in being 'insignificant' while everyone tries to be an achiever. He replied that truly speaking we all are insignificant and driven by our destiny as much as by our efforts. If we are aware of this, we'd be humble and grateful. Then as if to mock at me he said something I never knew:

the story of Sunil Gavaskar. Did you know that even Gavaskar, the legendary opening batsman would have been a fisherman had destiny not decided otherwise?"

Shyam's eyes widened in disbelief.

Venky got excited, "Gavaskar was born with a mark in his ear and his uncle had noted it. The next morning when his uncle again visited the hospital, he saw the child's ear had no mark. He instantly raised an alarm. After a frantic search, finally the little boy was seen in a fisherwoman's crib. The child was accidentally swapped during the daily baths. Had it not been for his uncle's alertness, the legendary Gavaskar that we know of today, would have probably been a fisherman. Gavaskar did work hard to be a master batsman, but remember destiny plays a role too, and because Gavaskar was aware of this, he is humble and grounded, and it's this humility that helped him attain worldly glory."

Shyam quipped, "Hmm....Gavaskar as a fisherman, I can't imagine, and I guess that's why Gavaskar, as a batsman, had a fetish for fishing outside the off stump!"

Shyam, in a reflective tone then said, "There's more to Aki. Last Sunday we were cleaning the plates and Aki was quietly doing his job. I was smiling to myself knowing that he had just returned from an international yoga conference in Chicago. I admired how he prefers to keep his mouth shut as he serves as a rank and file member of the ashram. As I basked in his presence, I was suddenly shaken.

"Our new janitor curtly demanded from Aki why he had missed the previous Sunday cleaning. I was taken aback by his audacity to question Aki but what amazed me was Aki's response; he was unperturbed by the reprimand and humbly apologized. Few moments later he asked for a leave of absence for the next Sunday as well. I know he's going to New Delhi to chair the global summit of 'Yoga for peace' convention but he didn't even hint about his senior position in the ashram. But the most touching moment for me was when later I asked him why he didn't clarify to the servant about his travels, he said he felt ecstatic at being treated as an ordinary member of the ashram. He then joyfully exclaimed that his plate cleaning service is now a success because he's being treated as a servant, and that's his real position! He often says we all are servants, and powers beyond us controls us at all times."

Shyam then smiled, "He told me sometime ago that better be humble voluntarily, because the world is anyways designed to humble us. He often says we never get what we want. Even if we do achieve our dreams, somethings will elude us, and no matter who we are, we will be humbled for sure. When I was distressed once, Aki comforted me with the example of Madhav Apte and Bradman. He said Madhav Apte was one of the best Indian batsmen who played a mere seven international matches and scored an impressive century against the best Westindies team. Yet, he was mysteriously dropped from the Indian team, and even sixty years later, nobody knows why he never played international cricket again. Life is tough, and you can't do anything about it. Bradman is another example. Considered as one of the greatest batsmen ever, he walked to play his last innings, and needed a mere four runs to average hundred in test cricket. Yet, in the very second ball he was bowled for a duck. Bradman was stunned. He slowly walked back to the pavilion, and he couldn't achieve that rare, special glory of averaging hundred. Aki says all the best cricketers-Gavaskar, Bradman and Tendulkar- have been sincere and hardworking, yet they have also been lucky. And destiny is a critical factor even in the lives of the strongest monks. Let's chose to be humble for our fleeting life is far beyond our own tiny plans and ambitions. We are instruments of God, meant for something higher and more sublime. That's why Aki finds the greatest joy in the simplest acts of cleaning toilets and washing pots. He's a true billionaire."

"And look at me, I cut corners during the Sunday services," Venky said, "But I do want to be wealthy like him."

❑ ❑ ❑